THE LARRABEE HEIRESS

The suit she had been wearing when the car struck her was inexpensive, not at all the sort of thing the wealthy Sandra Larrabee would wear. The keys that had been found in her handbag didn't fit any doors at the Larrabee mansion. The blond man who haunted her dreams bore no resemblance to Larry Larrabee, her late husband.

The Larrabees hadn't wanted to tell her, but at last they did. When Larry died, she had changed, become withdrawn and secretive. At the time of the accident she had been away from home for a week. Had she, before she lost her memory, been leading a double life? Was there a disreputable secret in her past that might some day embarrass her—or a dangerous one that might cost her her life?

THE
LARRABEE HEIRESS

DOROTHY DANIELS

WARNER BOOKS

A Warner Communications Company

WARNER BOOKS EDITION

Copyright © 1972 by Dorothy Daniels
All rights reserved

ISBN 0-446-88586-X

Cover art by Ben F. Stahl

Warner Books, Inc., 75 Rockefeller Plaza, New York, N.Y. 10019

Ⓦ A Warner Communications Company

Printed in the United States of America

Not associated with Warner Press, Inc. of Anderson, Indiana

First Printing: December, 1972

Reissued: December, 1977

10 9 8 7 6 5 4 3

THE LARRABEE HEIRESS

ONE

I was in my early twenties according to best professional guesses, but I was born seventy-five days ago in St. Bartholomew's Hospital. The name on the metal-weighted, brown vinyl-bound case history was Jane Doe. Today I was to learn who I was.

Until a week ago, I shared a two-bed, semi-private room with an assortment of patients who came and went. Then Dr. Beardsley brought in a strikingly handsome woman who stood at my bedside and studied me quietly. I heard her sharp intake of breath and saw her eyes film. Then she bent down and touched my brow in a light kiss. She blinked away the tears as she straightened and slipped her hand around mine, pressing it gently. After which she walked from the room, pausing momentarily at the door to turn and give me a last look as if to further reassure herself. A smile touched her lips, but I was too astounded to return it. I watched her walk briskly along the corridor until she passed beyond my view, and I noted how beautifully her mauve wool suit outlined her slender figure.

My eyes switched to Dr. Beardsley, standing at the foot

of my bed, his arms folded over his chest, looking pleased, even amused by my bewilderment.

"Who is she?" I asked.

"All in good time, my dear," he replied quietly.

"But she knows me," I exclaimed impatiently.

"Did you recognize her?" he asked.

"No." Much to my disgust I felt my eyes film. Then I added hopefully, "Perhaps if she'd spoken."

"I gave her orders not to say a word," he replied kindly. "I wanted to see if the sight of her would prod your memory even a little."

"It didn't," I replied tonelessly. "But I would still like to know who she is."

He moved up to the side of the bed and rested a reassuring hand on my shoulder. "Be patient, my dear. I want to talk further with her. I must be thoroughly convinced you are who she says you are. Even a slight disappointment might be dangerous to you in your present condition."

Not that I was diagnosed as unbalanced. Nobody ever insinuated that, and I felt quite normal except for one thing. My mind had become a complete blank as a result of having been run down by a car which mounted a sidewalk on Hollywood Boulevard.

Things changed after this woman's visit. I was moved to one of the rooms the nurses referred to as the Grand Suite because the windows were twice as large, the floor was thickly carpeted, there was a small wet-bar in one corner, four upholstered chairs, a twenty-one-inch color TV set and a lavish bathroom. Accompanying all this was a tab of a hundred and sixty dollars a day. A high tariff for a girl who had literally not a penny to her name— whatever the name was.

Today I sensed big things were going to happen, because the nurses deluged me with so much attention. I wondered if other patients on the floor were even given their breakfast and their pills.

For the moment, I was alone and I welcomed it. I spent some time looking out of the window at the Santa Monica Mountains which ringed much of Los Angeles. It was a crisp, cool and remarkably clear day; even the snow-capped San Gabriels were visible. On days like this, the natives look at the distant mountains and welcome them back while the newer residents are aghast at their first sight of them.

I wore a blue nightgown, compliments of my psychiatrist, Dr. Beardsley, who said it deepened the blue of my eyes. Over this was the regulation hospital gray robe. I went into the bathroom and stood before the full-length mirror. I was pale as a fresh bedsheet because I hadn't been outside in two and one-half months. They'd had to do some surgery on my skull, which meant my head had been shaved. The hair had grown in by now, however, but only into a kind of curly crewcut. Surprisingly, it was flattering in a freaky way and compensated for the rather drab brown color. My eyes were my best point, being a clear blue with no shading of color. The rest of my face was passable, though my retroussé nose didn't go with my angular features. I was slender, small-boned, of medium height and weighed one hundred and ten pounds.

But, I asked my reflection in the mirror, who was I? What was my background? Where did I come from and, more pertinent to the day, where was I going? The handsome woman who'd kissed me still remained anonymous. I'd have demanded to know her identity from Dr. Beardsley, but after her visit, he'd remained away from me until yesterday and even then told me I must be patient one more day, that he was almost satisfied, but wanted to make a final check. I was certain his practice was extensive and, not wishing to be difficult, I restrained my impatience until today when he promised he'd give me the information I desperately wanted.

But now that the day was at hand, I wasn't at all certain I wanted it. Or if I really wished to learn who I was. Here, feeling snug and safe in this hospital, with every wish granted me, I'd grown accustomed to being looked after and pampered. Even when I was in the semi-private room, the nurses and interns had given me excellent attention. I reasoned they were more compassionate for a girl who didn't know who she was, than for a patient going into labor, or being prepped for surgery. It would be pleasant and easy to stay here and let this way of life continue. Actually, I was afraid to go beyond the confines of these walls and face a world as alien to me as to a baby being born this minute downstairs in one of the delivery rooms.

So when Dr. Beardsley walked in, I didn't exult, or grow faint with excitement, or ask him a hundred questions. I merely sat down in one of the chairs and waited to hear what he had to say.

Dr. Beardsley was a corpulent, stubby little man with very keen eyes, not much hair, but possessed of a commanding nature probably developed from the practice of his profession. He was not a neurosurgeon, but a man I'd been turned over to so he might treat what was inside my head after the outside had healed. He was always crisply immaculate, with a ready smile and a friendly manner. Today, he seemed to radiate good cheer.

"Well now," he said, "are you ready to have the curtain raised?"

I managed a smile. "Yes, Doctor."

"You're mighty calm about it, I must say."

"Inwardly, I'm frightened, but I am who I am. I won't be able to change it, so I'm prepared to accept it. I do hope I'm not a—a criminal, or something."

"Certainly not. Let me recap a bit. You were picked up by an ambulance crew on Hollywood Boulevard. A car out of control had shot across the road, mounted the curb and knocked you down. There was a skull fracture that was very depressed and there was brain damage. You were given emergency treatment, watched for twenty-four hours, and when you did not regain consciousness, you were brought into surgery. There the damage was repaired, clots removed, the skull made whole and you returned to consciousness immediately after the anesthetic wore off. But you had no memory."

"I still haven't," I reminded him.

"True. This condition may be temporary or permanent. There is no way of knowing. It's what we call a retrograde amnesia—that is, the memory hiatus goes back into the period before the accident. I tried every known method of restoring your memory. We had a number of sessions during which you were subjected to long periods of hypnosis. Sometimes this works. In your case, it didn't make the slightest impression."

"Then you really have no further prognosis in my case," I said.

"None. We can't tell what will happen. Oh, you're fully restored to health and in no danger. There will be no aftereffects from the surgery or the accident, except for the loss of memory."

"So what happens next?" I asked.

He opened the case history which he'd been supporting on his lap. "The first thing to do is cross out the name Jane Doe." He drew a line through it with a flourish. "Now we write in the name of Sandra Larrabee."

"That's me?" I asked, savoring the name like a bit of filet mignon.

"That's you. Sound familiar?"

I shook my head. "Not in the least, Doctor."

"Well, I didn't expect it would. You no doubt recall the lady I brought in here to observe you last week."

I nodded. "Is she my mother?"

"No. Your mother-in-law. Her name is Janet Larrabee."

"I'm married?" My astonishment was evident in my voice.

"You're a widow. Your husband died eight months ago."

My poor mind was beginning a whirl that threatened to make me dizzy. "What about *my* family? I must have some blood relatives."

"Unfortunately you have none. Your parents have been dead for years and you were an only child. There aren't even cousins. However, on the Larrabee side, there are enough relatives to keep you from being lonely."

I said, "You know, Doctor, I asked myself over and over if it was possible I might be a married woman. Each time I rejected the idea as being inane. Now you tell me I *was* married. How can a girl forget a thing like that?"

"My dear, you've proved it possible."

"Yes," I admitted. "So my name is Sandra. I like it. What was it before my husband gave me the name of Larrabee?"

"Prentice. Sandra Prentice."

"Where was I from?"

"New York City. You came to Los Angeles five years ago, when you were eighteen."

11

"At least I know I'm twenty-three. Maybe I'll make this day my birthday. I'm certainly going to need one."

"No doubt your husband's people know your real birthday. Now I want you to have everything clear in your mind. You have not the slightest symptom of anterograde amnesia, the kind that results in loss of memory of things after a disturbance. I've tested you a dozen times. You will remember everything normally since the accident, but not before it. You might be lucky and have that memory return. I doubt it, but I won't rule it out."

"Darn the thief who stole my handbag after I was knocked down."

"Yes, because that bit of filching stopped us cold. Two teen-agers chased him, causing him to throw away the purse, but not before he'd looted it of everything it contained, except three keys on a key ring. Your mother-in-law has already taken it home."

My smile was ironic. "She can show me what doors they fit."

He leaned forward and patted my hand in a fatherly way. "You're taking it well. You always have, and that helps a great deal."

"To bring up more practical matters, who will pay your fee and the hospital bill which, I know, is astronomical by now?"

"It has all been paid for. The Larrabees, my dear Sandra, are not poor. Quite the opposite, as you'll discover. Now I'm going to leave. Next time I see you will be at your home. You may need treatments for some time." He consulted his watch. "In an hour, a car will call for you. You will be taken home and that's where you'll meet the people you should know, but don't. Mrs. Larrabee wanted it that way and I approved. The shock won't be quite as great. Bear up now. You have nothing but an extremely bright future to look forward to."

"A bright future with a blank past," I said. "I wonder how that will seem? Thank you for everything you've done. I'm grateful. But for the neurosurgeon and the fine people in this hospital who attended me, I might have died physically. But for your skill, I might now be dead mentally."

"You've been an interesting case and a fine patient,"

12

he said. "I've just one more word of advice. When you get home, hang onto your hat. You'll soon see what I mean. Good-bye for now, and good luck, Sandra."

I nodded and smiled and walked into the corridor with him. When I returned to my room, I closed the door and considered. Would I have to borrow the hospital robe to go home in? The moderately-priced tan suit I had been wearing at the time of the accident had one sleeve almost torn off and the remainder was rumpled because it had been blood-soaked and washed. One stocking was in shreds. My shoes, medium-heeled black pumps, were intact and my undergarments had come out of the wash well enough. My handbag, with three keys to my unknown past, was already at home. If I tried to leave the hospital in that suit, though, I'd probably be shunted into some psychiatric ward again. Still, a hospital robe. . . . About the time I decided I'd have to wear the suit, no matter what the consequences, a large package was delivered.

Inside the big box was the solution to my problem; a spring coat of sky blue Italian silk with a short-sleeved dress that matched the coat lining, a beautiful print on blue silk. There were navy blue pumps in my size, a blue leather handbag, plus the finest hose and undergarments. I had also been provided with a make-up kit. Everything it contained was just right for me.

I wondered if I'd been accustomed to such expensive garb, but the answer eluded me. Everything was a total blank on matters happening before I woke up in the recovery room. Yet my common sense told me I must have been, even though the suit which had been brought to me certainly wasn't in the same category. No matter. The Larrabees would fill me in on my life before the accident. At least, I hoped they could.

When I had finished dressing and surveyed myself in the full-length mirror, I was pleasantly impressed. The superb clothing fit perfectly, and I threw my old clothes into the wastebasket. I'd already checked them and knew there wasn't a mark on them with which I could be identified. My toothbrush, hair brushes and combs, little jars of face creams and some toilet water, comprised my luggage.

I looked about my room, still reluctant to leave the

refuge it had offered me. A discreet tap on the door announced the arrival of an orderly with a wheelchair. I, who had been roaming the corridors of the hospital for two months, had, by regulation, to use the wheelchair in leaving.

I said good-bye to the nurses, aides, and cleaning women on my way to the elevator. I was going home. I didn't know where home was, but that's where I was headed. The situation seemed as unreal to me as my past.

TWO

In the area provided for discharging patients, a single car waited, with a uniformed chauffeur, hat in hand, standing beside it. He was of medium height, with closely cropped gray hair and a face so seamed with wrinkles it was impossible to tell whether it was the result of age, heredity, or a life spent out of doors.

He smiled at sight of me and inclined his head slightly. "Miss Sandra. How well you look. It's good to see you again and know you've completely recovered."

"Thank you," I said. "But I haven't completely recovered, since I don't know your name. Or are you a new employee of the family?"

"Oh no, Miss Sandra. I'm Gilbert."

"Hello, Gilbert. Forgive my lapse of memory."

"I understand," he said kindly.

I turned to the orderly who stood ready to assist me into the car. "Thank you for bringing me down. I can manage nicely now."

Nonetheless he stood there dutifully until I got into the back seat and sat down in what I imagined to be about thirty thousand dollars' worth of luxury. It seemed to me

15

that Gilbert eased the car out of the driveway and onto the street without even starting the motor, until I realized it had been going all the time, but I couldn't hear it.

I grew more and more tense as the car turned onto Sunset Boulevard. Dr. Beardsley had warned me to hang on to my hat. After viewing the Rolls Royce, I was beginning to understand what he meant.

We left the congestion of Sunset Strip, rolled on into Beverly Hills, sailed by the Beverly Hills Hotel which I probably knew, but now I was aware of only by what I read on the sign designating it. We continued on, the road winding more and more, and the mansions disappearing behind hills and thick vegetation.

The car slowed, made a right turn onto a narrow driveway and came to a stop in front of a high, heavy gate set in a red brick fence. The chauffeur touched a button on the dash and the radio-controlled gate opened silently and unassisted. The car passed through and started up a moderate incline.

On both sides of me were sweeping lawns dotted with cleverly sculptured bushes. For a front lawn, it seemed endless. We reached a point where the slope ended and the driveway leveled off. I was faced with a mansion painted a gleaming white, three stories high, with a two-story wing on either side. The porch was wide, there were two side entrances. The approach was through a formal Italian garden, walled in by an arrangement of flower beds, flanked with statues and fountains.

The car floated to a stop before the main entrance. At the top of the fanstairs stood the handsome woman who had visited me. To one side of her stood an array of servants: two maids in uniform, a housekeeper identified by a crisp gray-and-white striped dress, and two men servants, probably gardeners, for they wore forest green uniforms.

Flanking Mrs. Larrabee on the other side stood an aristocratic-looking man, undoubtedly the master of this household. A young woman, plain in appearance, in her early twenties, was studying me solemnly. Beside her was another young lady who presented quite a different picture. She was a golden blonde, smartly dressed, poised and self-confident.

The chauffeur was holding the car door open, so I emerged and stood there. The woman came down the steps to greet me with both arms extended.

"Oh, my dear, it's good to have you back with us." Her smile was warm as she embraced me.

I said, "I'm both sorry and embarrassed that I don't know any of you. But first, do I really live here?"

"Live here?" Her soft laughter added to her attractiveness. "My dear Sandra, you own it."

"Dr. Beardsley warned me to hang on," I said wryly, "but I was ill-prepared for this."

"I know," she said understandingly. "I'm just hopeful that you'll slip into the routine of your former life so easily, your memory will gradually return."

Her manner was so warm I was fast losing my nervousness. I said, "Dr. Beardsley told me who you are, but will you please tell me yourself?"

"Certainly. And don't feel self-conscious because you don't remember. I'm Janet Larrabee, your mother-in-law."

"How did I address you?"

"You called me Janet," she replied. "I wanted you to call me *mater*. It was what Larry always called me, but you told me I looked too young for that. I thought it very kind of you, even though it wasn't the truth."

"You're a very beautiful woman," I said. I was certain she knew it, though I doubted she gave it too much thought, for her charm was her naturalness. I must have been very fond of her.

She took my hand and kept a grasp of it while she led me up the steps and presented me to her husband, Richard Larrabee—casually called Richie by all, I learned later. I took quick stock of him and I liked him on sight. His hair was going, but what was left was black, obviously dyed, for his brows were pure white over a pair of sharp gray-blue eyes. He was paunchy, but his posture was good, making it seem less noticeable. His skin was heavily tanned by California sunshine and, I suspected, sun lamps at this season of the year.

His voice was deeply masculine. "Dear Sandra, we've missed you."

"Dr. Beardsley and I had to restrain Richie from visiting you," Janet explained.

"The rules were foolish," he said. "But you're back with us now and that's what counts. I don't suppose you remember our daughter Nancy."

"I wish I could say I did." I turned to the young lady who had been eying me in an owlish manner. At close range I saw that she was what is termed, in a kindly way, a plain girl. She was angular and too thin. Her hair, as black as her father's, was center-parted and caught at the nape of her neck in a leather barrette. Her eyebrows were heavy, in need of care and black as her hair. By contrast, her face seemed a dead white which proper make-up could have softened. She wore a brown dress which hung from her shoulders to her ankles. It managed to conceal whatever figure she had.

"Welcome home, Sandra," she said quietly.

"Thank you, Nancy." She made no move to come to me, so I extended a hand in a gesture of friendship. Without taking a step, she leaned forward, grasped it lightly and, as quickly, released it.

There was no time for further conversation because the other girl, who scintillated from the top of her head to the tips of her toes, came to me. She looked like—gold? No, that was too hard. Golden sunshine was a better way to describe her. She smiled, revealing beautiful teeth to go with the laughing eyes and perfectly oval face. Her eyes were topaz and slanted upwards the merest bit at the outer corners. She was strikingly beautiful and her figure was slender, but curved in the proper places. She wore a sea-green woolen skirt and gold blouse. A wide belt accented a small waistline.

"I'm Marilyn, Nancy's sister. And, of course, Larry, your late husband, was our brother."

"Hello, Marilyn." I extended a hand as I studied her carefully, hoping for some stirring of memory, however slight. But she ignored the gesture and embraced me. "It's good to have you home again. You look well, but you're thinner. It's becoming though. So is the outfit I selected for you."

"Yes, it is," I agreed. "Thank you."

"It was a joy shopping for it, knowing you'd be coming back to us. We've missed you terribly."

"You're very kind," I said, wishing I could say the

18

same thing of them. With the exception of Nancy, they seemed genuinely glad to see me. I had no idea how she felt about me, for her features were noncommittal.

"I'll introduce you to the servants," Marilyn said. Before she brought me over, she told me in an undertone they were new with the exception of Ethel, the housekeeper, and Gilbert who'd brought me home.

Ethel was short, rotund, with a round face, a twinkle in her small button eyes and a smile of welcome widening her mouth. She embraced me, brushed a tear from the corner of her eyes, then took one of my hands between both of hers.

"Thank God you're home and well," she exclaimed, her voice quavering with emotion. "Almost well, Miss Sandra. I'll pray you get your memory back."

"Thank you, Ethel," I said gratefully. I realized I'd completely forgotten my nervousness in the warmth of the welcome I'd received.

She released her grip on my hand and Marilyn introduced me to Ava, the upstairs maid, and Dicie, the downstairs maid. The two men, Tom and Harry, did the gardening and any other chores which were required either in the house or on the grounds. Janet nodded to the servants in a gesture of dismissal, then motioned Marilyn and me inside. Richie and Nancy followed.

The reception hall was bigger than most ordinary homes. It was two stories in height and overlooked by a railed landing. There was a graceful curve to the wide staircase and above the curve was a stained-glass window. Two great chandeliers would provide light on state occasions.

"Remember the window?" Marilyn asked.

"No." I studied it solemnly. The sun was on it and sent shafts of vari-colored light down on us, giving the hall a cathedral-like air.

Marilyn said, "You loved it, and whenever you were about when I descended the stairway in daylight, you made me pause halfway down."

"I can reason that out," I said, regarding her, even now bathed in brilliant hues. "The colors make you look ethereal—as if you'd stepped from a painting."

"That's exactly what you used to say," she exclaimed.

19

I shifted my gaze to regard the window, hopeful it might stir my memory, but my attention was taken by the sight of two little girls, coming down the stairs, each about three years old and garbed in identical pink dresses. They were, of course, twins, and I wondered whom they belonged to. Their hair was fair, their eyes as blue as mine. When they reached the bottom, they paused and surveyed me solemnly. I noticed each had a name stitched in blue thread on a little pocket of the dress, but before I had an opportunity to read them, something happened which stunned me.

As if on signal, each of the little girls cried out "Mommy." The next instant, their faces wreathed in happy smiles, they ran to me, arms stretched upward for my embrace.

I was overwhelmed, but I knelt automatically and gathered them in my arms. Theirs enclosed my neck and they kissed me on the cheek. I kissed them in return, then looked up into Janet Larrabee's face. She was watching the tableau, her features hopeful.

A look of regret crept into her eyes and her voice as she said, "She doesn't remember them."

Nancy's smile was mocking. She seemed actually pleased at my bewilderment. Richie's features were thoughtful, Marilyn's sympathetic.

Janet said, "Sandra, these are your twin daughters, Carol and Christine."

I didn't rise from my kneeling position, nor did I release my hold on the children. My eyes surveyed the adult members of the family, then I regarded the little girls hopefully. Yet nothing stirred within me. I remembered no one in this house. The children in my arms were total strangers. I fought back tears and stood up, more than a little angry and thoroughly frustrated. At that moment I made a solemn vow to make every effort to regain my memory. I must. I didn't know where I'd begin, but I'd lose no time.

Then the thought occurred to me that this was my home. What better place was there to start?

THREE

Janet Larrabee took over then. "I think you should rest a while, Sandra. This has been a great shock. Yet it couldn't be avoided."

"I wouldn't want it to be—or even postponed," I said. "Though I'm glad I didn't know about," I glanced down at the twins, each of whom held one of my hands and was regarding me curiously, "everything—or anything."

Marilyn said, "Dr. Beardsley thought it would be better that way."

Janet said, "Ava will take the children out to their play yard. We kept them in until you came so they'd be fresh and clean. They are mischievous little girls and manage to get quite dirtied up."

Ava descended the stairs. Apparently she'd been standing at the landing, ready to take over their responsibility once they'd welcomed me home. She was no more than twenty-five and looked quite trim in her beige uniform. Her square face was topped with black hair cropped short, revealing a well-shaped head. The children went to her willingly, transferring their grip from my hand to hers. Her smile for them was one of reassurance, and as they moved down the long hallway to the rear of the house, they started chattering about what they wanted to do. She laughed softly and must have made an appropriate reply, for the children squealed with delight.

When they were out of earshot, I said, "Not knowing about *them* hurts the most. How could anyone forget having children?"

Marilyn said cheerfully, "They might be the instrument which will help restore your memory."

"I hope so," I said. "But I shan't depend only on them. I'm determined to do everything to get complete recall of my past."

Janet's arm encompassed my waist. "We'll help all we can. Now come upstairs. I'll show you your suite."

My smile was apologetic. "You'll have to."

"We understand. Dr. Beardsley told us your amnesia is complete."

"It must be, since I didn't even recognize my own daughters—two of the loveliest little girls I've ever seen."

Janet spoke as she led me up the stairs. "We had their names stitched on their dresses and jackets and sweaters, as an aid to you."

"I noticed. It was good of you."

We reached the top of the stairs and I paused to look down at the trio. I felt a little giddy from the height, but I also felt reassured when Richie nodded and a smile of encouragement touched his lips. Marilyn blew me a kiss. Nancy's smile was gone and her features were now devoid of expression. I wondered if she resented my presence in the house and if so, why.

Janet and I proceeded down a wide corridor which apparently led to the east wing of the house. There she opened a door and I entered the sitting room of what I soon learned was my three-room suite. What I had here was a miniature house of my own. The sitting room was large, done in soft green throughout with a comfortable-looking chaise-longue before the fireplace.

The next room was a small den equipped with a desk, another fireplace, and two oversized leather chairs. Over the mantel hung an old portrait of a handsome young man in evening dress. He was dark-haired, slim, athletic looking, with regular features.

22

I glanced at Janet. "Is he . . . ?"

"My son," she said. "Your late husband. We'll talk about him as soon as you've seen your bedroom."

It was breathtaking, done in white without a trace of another color. Somehow, I felt I'd have liked a splash of orange or crimson to relieve the effect of its stark whiteness. It was a beautiful room though, with a canopied four poster, a triple dresser, and white velvet chairs scattered about. Matching draperies framed the windows. One wall was mirrored, making the large room seem enormous. An adjoining powder room had a long make-up table beneath a windowed wall. The bath was beyond and a glance revealed more whiteness, except for the black enameled sink, toilet, tub, and a shower tiled in black. I walked back through the bedroom, regarding the rug, as white as the velvet bedspread. I supposed if one could afford to live in a mansion like this, the expense of having the rug cleaned frequently was of no importance.

We returned to the sitting room where Janet insisted I stretch out on the chaise longue. I gave her no argument, for the shock of knowing I was the mother of twins had left me shaken. She took a chair opposite me and began to talk.

"Now I shall try to fill you in. Enough to keep you from the confusion you feel at present. But please don't be discouraged. Just remember, each of us will help in whatever way we can to lift the cloud from your mind which is blocking all memory of your past."

I looked about the room. "If only one little item stirred my memory."

Janet leaned forward and patted my hand reassuringly. "We were hopeful something would. That's why Dr. Beardsley wouldn't even give you a hint of what was in store for you and wouldn't allow me a return visit or even to speak to you that one day he allowed me to see you. And he questioned each of us for hours on end to make certain you were who we said you were."

Somehow, knowing that, I felt better. "Then I really belong here."

"If Dr. Beardsley had the slightest doubt, we'd not be having this little conversation now. But to get on with it. My son, Larry, met you in New York. He visited a friend

23

for whom you worked as secretary and fell in love with you. That night he telephoned and said he'd be delayed in coming home because he'd not leave until you consented to marry him."

"You mean it was a brief courtship?" The thought occurred to me that I must be an impulsive individual— as impulsive as Larry who, as of now, was just the name of a gentleman whose portrait hung over the mantel in the small den.

Her smile was tolerant. "Very brief, and though I felt concern, I also knew my son and the qualifications he sought in a woman he would choose to spend the rest of his life with. Believe me, my dear, when he returned with you as his bride four years ago, my concern vanished immediately. It was as if we'd known one another all our lives. I felt I'd gained another daughter, and I hope I don't sound trite."

My smile was pleased. "It sounds wonderful. What happened to my—to Larry?"

Her face shadowed momentarily. "Don't be afraid or hesitant about referring to him as your husband. You were a devoted couple. It might eventually prove a help rather than an embarrassment."

I could see the logic to her statement. "Very well. What happened to my husband?"

"He developed a brain tumor. It grew so rapidly he never had a chance. In three months he was dead. That's why we worried so about you. And why we obeyed Dr. Beardsley's admonition that you were not to have visitors."

"I can't remember," I said forlornly. "I can't remember anything." I arose and walked to a long table equipped with three shallow drawers. I opened the middle one and deposited my purse and gloves inside.

"You haven't forgotten everything," Janet said.

I turned around. "What do you mean?"

"You always placed your purse and gloves in that drawer. As you did a moment ago without even thinking."

I was amazed but comforted, though I had no recollection of ever having done so.

Janet went on. "A small item, but it pleases me and it will Dr. Beardsley. Now about your accident. There's no need to dwell on it, since Dr. Beardsley told us he's

24

already discussed it with you and he's given us explicit instructions about how we should treat you."

I smiled. "I hope I'll be treated as one of the family."

"Oh, of *course*. What I mean is, he wants a cheerful atmosphere at all times so you'll feel safe and secure."

"I hope I'll not give you any problems."

She smiled reassuringly. "You certainly seem normal. I'm relieved."

Her statement puzzled me. "Wasn't I always?"

Her brow furrowed. "I may as well tell you that prior to your disappearance, you did give us cause for concern. So much so, we had a private detective shadow you. But you learned about it and became quite clever at eluding him. However, he did discover that you had, some time prior to your disappearance, gone to a travel agency and purchased a ticket for a cruise around the world. We contacted the ship, but they had no record of you coming aboard and the ticket you'd bought hadn't turned up. We still thought you were aboard, perhaps under an assumed name."

"Why should I have done that? Gone off without letting you know?"

"My dear Sandra, I am of the opinion that all of your memory loss is not due entirely to the accident. You . . . well, you were not yourself after Larry died. You locked yourself in these rooms and refused to come out. We had to beg you to eat. When you finally did emerge, it was to go off by yourself, at first for hours, then for days. One time you were gone a week. That's why, during the last disappearance, we didn't immediately evidence too much concern for you. Also, we feared we might antagonize you and you would leave us and desert your daughters whom we knew you loved dearly."

"I'd have been less than human to feel otherwise," I said, puzzled and vaguely offended.

"You weren't yourself, Sandra. You withdrew completely, keeping to your suite most of the time. On the rare occasions when we succeeded in coaxing you downstairs to join us in a cocktail before dinner, you never entered the conversation. You didn't even sip your drink. You merely held your glass, staring at its contents as if you had no idea of what the glass contained."

25

"Didn't I even join you at the table?" I asked.

"No, dear. Ethel brought a tray up to you and sat with you to make certain you ate."

"Was I rude or abusive?"

"Certainly not," Janet said and for the first time a note of sternness crept into her voice. "You were a warm, loving young woman and you still are. However, the shock of Larry's death affected you to a much greater extent than it did us and we were resolved to do nothing to antagonize you lest you leave us. There were the twins, you know. We knew you loved them and though, during that period, you ignored them, we feared that one time you might take them with you. We loved them too and we didn't want to lose them—or you."

My smile was apologetic. "Thank you for having been so understanding."

Janet made a disparaging gesture with her hand and I noticed how beautiful it was—the slender, tapering fingers, the nails medium long, exquisitely manicured.

"Why shouldn't we have been?" she exclaimed. "Larry's death, so cruel and sudden, was a terrible blow to the family, but it hit you the hardest, which is understandable. You were both so deeply in love. Usually in a marriage, one loves more than the other. But not in yours."

"I'm shocked by my behavior, particularly as regards the children."

She touched my arm comfortingly. "If you are truly sincere about regaining your memory, you mustn't fill yourself with guilt feelings."

I digested this slowly—so my behavior *had* been dreadful—and started to deal with the present. "Just what is my position in this house?"

"You own it. You inherited everything from our son."

"I hope you'll forgive me if I say it's a little too much for me to grasp."

She looked puzzled. "Why should it be?"

"It would seem that you and Richie must have some interest in the house or the holdings of the family. It's obvious great wealth is represented here."

Her smile was apologetic. "I forget everything must be explained to you. Larry's grandfather created the family fortune. His son Richie took no interest in finance or

26

the business world. I'll be honest—he was a playboy. And I was and still am a social butterfly. Our marriage has been a good one and a happy one, for we both like the same things. Larry, however, was a serious type and his grandfather developed a great fondness for him. In turn, Larry developed a keen liking for the world of finance. That pleased his grandfather, who had created an empire —several, I might say. He was not unscrupulous, but he was ruthless. To compensate for that, at least in my opinion, Larry had a brilliant mind for business and finance with none of the ruthlessness of his grandfather. Anyway, Larry was left the family wealth in its entirety. It made no difference really. Certainly not so far as Larry was concerned. Nor as far as we were concerned. Our lives went on as before. In fact, Larry increased our allowance substantially and turned over the running of the house to me."

"I'm glad," I said.

"At Larry's death, you became the sole heir. The will stipulated there was no need to provide for the children in the will because of your great love for them. It was a simple will, leaving everything to you."

"Who took care of things while I was ill?"

"Sidney Burwell, Marilyn's husband. He's an attorney."

"I didn't know Marilyn was married."

"Oh yes," Janet said, looking pleased.

"Is Nancy?"

"No, I'm sorry to say."

"Why should you be sorry?" Since her look was one of shocked surprise at my question, I added quickly, "What I mean is, it's no disgrace not to be. Perhaps she's never met anyone she cared about."

"She's never made the effort," Janet said. "She takes no interest in clothes or dressing her hair. Though she's not the beauty her sister is, she could make herself attractive. I've tried in tactful and discreet ways to help her, but she resents my efforts. I'm afraid Richie and I were cruel, without intending to be, when we christened Marilyn our golden girl."

I nodded. "It probably hurt Nancy deeply, even though you hadn't meant it to. I imagine she's older than Marilyn."

"Indeed not," Janet replied briskly. "Marilyn is two years older. She's been married three years and takes after me. Loves parties, travel, and interesting people who do things. I've given up on Nancy. She's interested in only one subject—protozoology."

"Well, at least she keeps her mind occupied."

Janet smiled. "The only time I've seen her glow is when she's observing her microscopic creatures that buzz around in a drop of water. She maintains a laboratory of sorts in a small shed behind the house. We had it built for her because we were afraid she'd blow up the main house with the chemicals she had stored on her shelves."

"How wonderful she has a hobby."

"For her it's perfect. I think she cares far more for those ugly bugs than she does us. Richie is quite discouraged with her because of that, though he's never voiced his disapproval to her. Now Marilyn is so different. You'd scarcely believe they could be sisters. Marilyn, as I said, is two years older than Nancy, but everyone believes she's five years younger. A gay, lively girl who likes and is liked by everyone. I don't need to go into more detail. You've talked with both my daughters. You knew them well, of course, though you've no memory of the past."

"Not even a glimmer," I confessed.

"Don't be discouraged. Dr. Beardsley impressed on us the fact that we must not expect a miracle. Patience and time will reap its own reward."

"I hope so."

"You've yet to meet Marilyn's husband, Sidney Burwell. He's outdoorsy and goes off on frequent fishing and hunting trips. He'll be returning today from the latter. He's a lawyer and accountant. Handles the estate for us. For you, now. Does well at it, though it's really under the supervision of some banks, as I understand it. These matters are too complicated for me."

"The very thought of it terrifies me," I said. "I can't imagine myself being able to converse intelligently about stocks or holdings of any kind."

"You won't need to just now," Janet consoled. "Nor do we want you to have that kind of responsibility just yet. Dr. Beardsley said you are to go slowly."

"Not too slowly," I said. "I'm determined to lift the

curtain on my past, though I'll try not to be a nuisance while doing so. I only hope you and the rest of the family won't mind my asking lots of questions."

"We want to help," Janet said. "I'll stay with you every moment if you wish."

"Thanks," I said gratefully. "But that would be a crutch and might delay my recovery."

"I agree," she replied kindly. She took a cigarette from a box on the table and lit it. I wondered if I smoked. There was much I had to learn about myself.

"I haven't thanked you for sending me the beautiful outfit I'm wearing."

"Yes, you did. Downstairs. But that was no problem. We knew your size and also your taste."

I shook my head negatively.

"What is it?" Janet asked.

"It's frightening to have others know things about me I have no awareness of." I touched the fabric appreciatively. "Somehow I can't believe I ever had anything of this quality before. Certainly, the garment I tossed into the wastebasket wasn't of the same grade of fabric."

"I didn't see it," Janet replied. "But then, you'd left here fully a week before the accident."

"What kind of car did I drive?"

"You didn't drive," Janet said, "because that day Marilyn persuaded you to come shopping with her. She wished to purchase dresses for Carol and Christine's birthday. For the first time since Larry died, you seemed more like yourself. Marilyn drove that day. You expressed a desire to go to Bullock's Westwood to make the purchase. Marilyn also wished to buy a scarf. You told her you would meet her in the children's department. When she went there, you were nowhere in sight. When she described you to the salesladies on the floor, they couldn't recall having seen you."

I pressed my hands to my temples in a vain effort to force some recollection of that day.

Janet stood up and rested a hand on my shoulder. "Don't try too hard, Sandra. You'll only upset yourself. Come back into the bedroom so I can show you where your clothes are."

I followed her and discovered the mirrored wall concealed a closet the size of a room. Janet touched a light switch inside the door. Glass enclosed shelves revealed purses and handbags and shoes. A row of hooks held belts ranging from evening to sportswear. The racks held dresses, coats, slacks outfits, blazers and blouses. It was like a boutique. I was aghast at the size of my wardrobe.

I gestured toward the racks. "These are mine?"

Janet nodded. "You loved clothes and had excellent taste. But then, I've noticed that New York girls who go to business are the best dressed in the country. At least, that's my opinion. I think it's always been that way."

I walked slowly back to the bedroom, followed by Janet.

"I feel like a person drowning. I can't seem to get my breath or my bearings."

"It's been a terrible ordeal for you. You were gravely ill and for a while your recovery was doubtful. Your accident, following so closely on Larry's death, was bound to have an effect on you. You were headed for a breakdown, which we were too stupid to realize. Your mind couldn't accept your loss, and you were trying to escape from reality. That's what Dr. Beardsley said. The accident did what you couldn't do."

I went to Janet, embraced her lightly and touched my cheek to hers. "Thank you for all you've done."

"We did nothing."

"You looked after my little girls and you're being very kind and patient in explaining everything to me. It's difficult to grasp it all, but I'm trying."

"You're over the worst of it. But you must rest. Your eyes have dark circles beneath them and you look tired."

"I am," I confessed.

"Get out of your clothes and slip into bed so you can really relax."

"Thank you, Janet."

Before she left, she went to one of the windows and slipped her hand behind the draperies. I heard a soft whirring and watched as they closed, plunging the room into darkness. It was a blessed relief, for I found the completely white room unnerving.

She said, "There's also a switch beside your bed to

open and close the drapes and another which turns the lamps on and off. I'll close the door to the den so you'll have quiet and complete darkness."

She kept the door open only long enough for me to find the switch. I snapped the one nearest me. Slow light filtered through the room. I relaxed and returned to the closet, selecting a pink chiffon negligee. I removed my clothes, hung them in the closet and went back to the bedroom. I removed the velvet coverlet from the pillows, snapped off the light switch and used the bedspread as a cover.

My body seemed to sag with weariness. I thought I was at ease here, but what I'd learned since my return had made me tense, though I realized the reason for much of it was exhaustion.

I felt myself drifting off to sleep. I don't know if the recurring dream I'd been having came immediately, or if I'd been asleep for some time, but there he was again, and the sight of him made me happy. Not that he was handsome. His features were too craggy for that. But his eyes had a way of looking into mine, as if he felt I were someone special. He was smiling back and he nodded briefly, as if telling me everything was going to be all right.

His hair was so blond it appeared to have been bleached by the sun and I had the feeling he was tall. Certainly his shoulders were broad and it would have been nice to rest my head on them.

He was still with me when I started to come awake and I recalled the events of this day. I wondered if, somehow, he was mixed up in my shattered past. Had I known him at one time? Had I ever been in love with him? Or had he been my employer in New York—the friend of Larry's?

Whoever he was, he had been in my dreams frequently. Sometimes on successive nights I would dream of him, yet I couldn't recall knowing him. But for some reason, I felt I'd known him somewhere and I sensed the relationship had been pleasant. Whenever I recalled his smile, I was certain of it.

FOUR

I came awake slowly and with an awareness that someone had switched on the lights. I opened my eyes, keeping
my lids lowered until my vision had accustomed itself to
the soft illumination. My head was turned toward the
door leading into the den. I recalled Janet had closed it,
but now it was open. I lay on my back and had only
to move my head slowly to scan the room.

Nancy was seated in a chair which she'd placed at my
bedside. On her lap was a large volume and her arms
rested on it. She was leaning forward slightly, her myopic
eyes studying me. At least, that was the impression I got.

She said, "Mama told me to waken you. Dinner is at
seven-thirty."

"What time is it, Nancy?"

"Six-thirty," came the laconic reply.

"I'll get dressed at once."

"I should really hate you," came her startling reply.

My hand had lifted the spread to toss it aside, but I
paused in bewilderment. "Hate me? Why?"

"You know why."

"I haven't the faintest idea of what you're talking

about." I made no attempt to keep annoyance from my voice.

"Oh, that's right. You don't remember anything. Or are you faking?"

"Faking? If you're trying to be funny, I don't appreciate your sense of humor."

"You mean you're on the level—you really don't know who you are?"

"I know only what I've been told—that I'm Sandra Larrabee."

She nodded and shrugged her shoulders, as if she didn't care one way or the other.

I eyed her speculatively. "Don't you believe I am?"

She nodded a second time. "I just wondered if you'd really lost your memory or were playing a joke on the family."

"Why should I play a joke on the family?"

"Because you're not a particularly nice person—at least, that's my opinion."

I was shaken by her statement. Certainly, she didn't seem to be lying, and I'd sensed her dislike for me downstairs when we met.

"What is there about me you don't like?" I asked.

"You were always making fun of me. Belittling me, telling me I had about as much appeal as an oil well."

"Oh, Nancy, I didn't," I exclaimed.

"You did. And Marilyn agreed. Even Mother has given up on me. Not that I blame her. But I don't want to be glamorous or 'mod' or doing the 'in' thing. I just want to be me—Nancy Larrabee."

"There's nothing wrong with that. I respect you for your individualism."

She looked skeptical. "It's the first time you ever said anything like that to me."

"For anything I said before the accident, I apologize."

"That's a switch. But thanks. Maybe the accident changed you."

"If I was what you say, I hope so."

"I guess I shocked you by telling you this."

I sat up and swung my legs over the side of the bed. "You shocked me all right. I want to take a bath, Nancy. You'll have to excuse me."

33

"Mind if I stay and talk while you dress?"

"Not at all."

She opened the textbook and was immediately absorbed in it. I went into the bathroom, once again marveling at its luxury. I decided on a shower. It would be quicker. I shampooed my hair, reveling as the needle shower massaged my scalp. I toweled myself briskly and ran my fingers through my short, wet curls, wrapped the oversize towel around me, and went back to the bedroom.

"Your undergarments are in the second drawer, center section of the triple bureau." She spoke without raising her head from her book.

I thanked her, repressing a smile, wondering how she knew. As if sensing my unspoken question, she said, "I looked in the drawers while you were sleeping. Everything is just as it was when you left. Do you know where the closet is?"

"Your mother showed me." I slid open the mirrored door, snapped on the light and chose a red dress with matching suede shoes. I returned to the bedroom, selected undergarments and stockings and dressed. Nancy was once again immersed in her book. At least, that's what I thought until she spoke, which she did without taking her eyes from the page.

"How do you like Father?"

"I scarcely know him. At least, as of today. I suppose I liked him before the accident."

"He's a fraud. Wants everyone to think he has all the money, but he hasn't a sou. He was completely dependent on Larry. All of us were. Your costume jewelry is in the tall chest with the narrow drawers. You only liked fake jewelry, but expensive fake. And you have a mess of it."

"I don't want to wear any tonight." I regarded my reflection in the full-length triple mirror which was angled against one corner of the room.

Nancy closed the book, cradled it in her arms and stood up slowly. I turned from the mirror to face her.

"You look beautiful just as you are," she said. "I like your hair."

"It's just growing in," I said. "My scalp was shaved, you know."

"I didn't know. Sid will like your new look."

34

"Sid?"

"Marilyn's husband, Sidney Burwell. He's one of those perennial juveniles. The tennis-player type. Away a lot hunting and fishing. But he's handsome and Marilyn loves him. I guess that's all that matters."

"It is, Nancy," I said, my tone slightly hostile. I wasn't at all certain I liked this girl. Not just because she was constantly on the defensive, but she seemed to have a knack for needling.

She again attempted the shrug, but not successfully this time, hampered as she was by the heavy volume. She said, "Would you like to see my digs?" I thought I detected a shy eagerness in her voice, though I must have been mistaken. "Not that you haven't been there before," she went on, "but you don't remember it. Of course, my room isn't like yours. I'm not the type for this, and one of the rooms is full of empty shelves. Mother put her foot down on having a lab in the house, so Larry made me one outside. Larry was good to me. He was really a brother. He's the one member of the family I loved. I didn't even want to live after he died."

"I'm sure it was a shock to the entire family—including me."

"Ready?" she asked.

I wondered if she'd lost interest in the subject, or disagreed with my statement.

"You have lots of make-up in the powder room, but there's more in the top drawer, right section," she motioned with her hand to the bureau.

"Thanks." I opened the drawer and saw several lipsticks lying in a neat row. I rejected two as having too much orange and chose a clear red.

"You don't use much make-up, do you?"

"I'm not sure," I said flippantly. "At the moment, all I want is a touch of lipstick. My cheeks have enough color."

She nodded agreement, said, "Let's go," and led the way from the room. I clicked out the light switch and followed her.

We'd started our walk down the corridor when I came to an abrupt halt and indicated a door on my left.

"I want to stop here for a moment."

"Why?" Nancy asked.

I smiled. "It was once Larry's room."

"How do you remember?"

"I don't. Am I right?"

Nancy said, "Open the door and find out."

I did and walked into a small room which had once been a nursery. There were boy's toys on shelves and overflowing a large toy box. Little had apparently been changed here since Larry grew up.

"It's just as it always was," Nancy said.

"Yes . . . just the same," I said.

"How'd you know this was Larry's room as a child?"

I stared at her blankly. "I have no idea. But I knew exactly what was behind this door." I grasped her arm in an impulsive gesture. "Oh, Nancy, my memory is beginning to come back."

Nancy said, "Wait'll Mother hears this."

"Let's go downstairs. I'll see your room later. I want to tell her."

"Go ahead. I want to put my book away."

I felt a surge of happiness the likes of which I hadn't experienced in a long time. I suppose Larry had shown me this room—or, more likely, his mother. I'd probably visited it several times. Certainly some of its contents were familiar. For sentimental reasons his mother had left it untouched.

I went downstairs in a daze, my heart pounding with excitement. Marilyn, Janet, and Richie met me at the landing. Apparently, they'd been awaiting me. We went into the dining room, but on the way I told them. It was impossible to keep the news to myself.

"Wonderful," Janet exclaimed.

Marilyn embraced me. "Didn't I tell you I knew things would come back quickly once you were home?"

"Yes," I said. I was bursting with happiness even though I was on the verge of tears I knew I must not give way to.

Richie said, "A pity Sid couldn't make it for dinner. We'd have a real family celebration."

"We'll have it anyway," Janet declared. Her arm around my waist, she led me into the dining room.

Twin candelabras flanked a bowl of fresh flowers on

the table. The lace cloth was exquisite, as were the china, silver, and crystal. Two other candelabras set on a long buffet. Two walls were mirrored, adding to the elegance of the room. Dicie served dinner, supervised unobtrusively by Ethel who came into the room from time to time. Talk centered around Larry, with Richie and Janet relating various incidents of our marriage, but I had no recall in regard to them. None of us were discouraged, however, because each of us felt I'd made a start.

Only Nancy remained aloof and I felt that, in her opinion, my memory lapse was still highly suspect. Yet I couldn't understand why she would feel that way. Certainly, she too should have exhibited pleasure, yet her manner was almost one of indifference. I knew then she still didn't like me. I reminded myself that I couldn't blame her if I'd been unkind to her and, unless she was a liar, I had been.

Not until coffee had been served did I remember the twins and I berated myself aloud for my forgetfulness.

Janet said, "Ava serves their meals in the playroom adjacent to their bedroom. Why don't you go up and say good night to them? They must be about ready to be tucked in."

I excused myself and went upstairs. Ava greeted me with a smile and the twins squealed with delight at my entrance. My heart warmed at the way their pretty faces lit up at sight of me, and I knew they'd been expecting me. I apologized for being late and asked that they be patient with me.

"Don't you remember us?" one of them asked.

"Of course I do, but you're so alike I can't tell which of you is Carol and which is Christine."

They giggled and one of them carefully identified herself. "I'm Carol and you can tell because I've got a mark right here." She pointed to a small mole on her left temple.

"Well, now I know. Tell me what you did today."

"Played," Christine said. "We thought you would come see us."

"I know I should have, but I had to rest after coming home from the hospital. I'll make it up to you. Tomorrow you'll have to take me around the estate and tell me about everything."

"Okay," Christine said.

"Don't you remember anything?" Carol asked, still intrigued by that problem.

"I'm afraid not very much. But with your help we'll soon see that I do. Okay?"

"Okay, Mommy," Carol said.

She'd called me Mommy. It sounded strange and alien. I felt nothing and I was ashamed of myself to a point where I made a great fuss over them and finally got them tucked in. I dimmed the lights and talked to them about such serious matters as having a doll carriage repaired, planning a party for them, encouraging them to tell me about their swings and chutes and tree house, located somewhere on the estate. Apparently I used to go there and play with them because they spoke of the area as if I should be familiar with it.

I noticed that Christine was the more loquacious one of the two, though they were both excited over my return and by my renewed promise, and it took them a long time to settle down.

Finally, I headed for the door, believing the light switch would plunge the room into darkness, but Carol anticipated me, for she said, "Don't forget to light the bunny."

I looked around, but didn't see a sign of it. Both girls giggled.

"It's not in the same place," Christine said.

"Where did it used to be?" I asked.

"Don't you remember?" Carol asked.

"I'm sorry, dear. I don't remember anything. You'll have to help me until I recover from the sickness of not remembering."

Carol said, "It used to be on the toy chest beneath the window, but it fell off and broke."

"You knocked it off," Christine said.

"I didn't mean to," Carol said solemnly.

"Well, Grandma got us another," Christine said serenely. "It's in that corner on the floor."

I walked to the far end of the room, directed by Christine's outstretched arm, with finger pointing downward. On the floor stood a large glass bunny with oversized ears, wide eyes, and enormous grin.

Christine said, "You press the button on his toe to light it."

I did and soft light emanated from it. The back of the lamp was open and when I stood up, I could see that the bulb was small and would give the room muted light.

I blew the girls a good-night kiss, went to the door, snapped the switch and the room was plunged into darkness, except for the little bunny whose light would be apparent once their eyes had adjusted.

They called a good night and I answered. As I closed the door, I wondered why I hadn't taken them in my arms and embraced them. Uneasiness gripped me as I also wondered how strong the mother instinct in me was.

FIVE

I was eager to return to the group, for only in that way would I get to know them again. And I hoped some comment they made or a casual phrase might drop that would jog my memory. I heard laughter and raised voices as I moved along the hall and smiled, wondering if my return had anything to do with their cheerfulness.

However, the reason for their vivaciousness was Sidney Burwell, Marilyn's husband, to whom I was introduced as soon as I entered the drawing room. He was well over six feet tall, firm of flesh and perfectly proportioned. He wore slacks, a loose-fitting suede jacket over a turtleneck sweater. He was handsome, with dark brown eyes, olive skin, a pencil-slim mustache and a smile which revealed beautiful white teeth.

Before anyone had a chance to say a word, he turned, set his half empty glass down, and extended both arms as he approached me.

"Sandra, dear, you look splendid. Sorry I wasn't here to welcome you. I'd intended to be, but the damn flight was delayed one hour. Rumors there was a bomb aboard."

"False, I hope," Richie said.

"Apparently," Sid replied. His hands lightly clasped my shoulders and he gave me a very chaste kiss on the brow. Then he released me and returned to his glass, taking a deep gulp from it.

"Hello, Sid," I said quietly. "At least, I presume that's how I addressed you."

"How else, since that's my name?" he said, giving me a mischievous wink. "That's a devilishly cute hair style. Did you get it free with the surgery?"

"That was part of it," I parried.

"Seriously, it's damn good to have you back with us," he said.

Janet moved to my side. "Come over here and sit down."

She led me to one of two divans which flanked the fireplace and drew me down beside her. Marilyn was curled in a corner of the one facing us. Richie leaned against the mantel, taking in the scene, looking very much the lord of the manor. He seemed to enjoy his father image and I gathered this was a happy, closely united family. Except for Nancy, who didn't seem to fit into any part.

At the moment, she was over by the window, looking out into the night.

Marilyn said proudly, "Sid got one deer and half a dozen partridge."

"He gave the deer away and he didn't bother to pick up the partridge." Nancy spoke from her place by the window and without turning around.

"Nancy, honey," Sid chided, "don't be such a spoil-sport."

"It's the truth, isn't it?" she retorted.

Sid shrugged. "So it's the truth. Who likes venison? And pheasant meat is too strong for my tastes. The partridge were picked up by other hunters. I'm sure they were eaten."

"Stop picking on Sid," Marilyn said good-naturedly.

Sid walked over to the divan, drew Marilyn from her corner and cradled her in his arms. His eyes thanked her for siding with him as he said, "Nancy knows I go for the exercise and not the food. Good to be back with you, baby. Beautiful baby."

Sid's voice was a drawl and I imagined he came from

the South. Marilyn's eyes were soft with her love for him. I had the feeling that he could do or say no wrong so far as she was concerned. And he felt the same way. I believed, from the way they were regarding each other, they'd completely forgotten our presence. But the tartness of Nancy's voice and the words she spoke brought them out of their reverie.

"I'm sure the deer and the birds appreciate your flat belly," Nancy said. "Excuse me. I think I'm going to vomit."

She stalked out of the room. Sidney smiled at her retreating back. "Nancy's all right. She can't get used to the fact that man is a predatory animal. Well, Sandy, the house will be livened up with you back. It's been as dull as an empty warehouse. We'll have to resume our never-ending tennis match."

"Tennis?" I said. "Did I play tennis?"

"You forget, Sid," my mother-in-law said. "Sandra has lost her memory and I should think something as inconsequential as tennis would be among the last things she'd remember."

"I'm sorry, Sandy," he said. "Even if you could remember, I doubt you'd feel much like playing."

"I'm sure she wouldn't," Marilyn said. "I'm afraid you'll have to settle for me as a partner."

He kissed her brow. "No hardship. Just so long as I don't have to play with your father."

Richie laughed and shrugged. "So I'm getting old."

"Not that old," Sid relented, smiling up at him.

"A left-handed compliment, but thanks anyway."

The repartee was good-natured and the feeling in the room one of strong family ties once Nancy had left. It was almost as if she hated all of them, even though none of them bore her any ill-will. At least, not that I could detect.

Sid said, "Did the twins remember you?"

I smiled. "They seemed to. I feel terrible, not remembering them."

"No reason for it," Sid said kindly. "But I'll lay odds they'll be the ones to poke your memory into wakefulness."

"I hope so," I said. "I do feel at ease with them. I just don't feel like a mother."

42

"You will," Janet said. "Because at one time you were a very loving and devoted mother. It will come back."

"You've already remembered two things," Marilyn said. "Where you used to place your purse and, more important, Larry's room when he was a child."

"Do the twins ever use it?" I asked.

Marilyn gave her mother a tolerant glance. "Mother won't let them. That's her shrine."

"He was my only son," Janet said quietly. "After his death, that room became hallowed."

"Your shrine to your son," Marilyn said. "A good thing the rooms Nancy and I shared weren't held in such reverence. The twins would have had to share the suite with Sandra and Larry."

Sid playfully smacked Marilyn's derrière. "Behave yourself. You sound jealous."

Marilyn snuggled her head beneath Sid's chin and sighed happily. "I was, but now that I have you, I've forgiven Mother."

Janet's laughter had the softness of a dove cooing. "I didn't desert either of my daughters. You got mother love just as Larry did."

"Not as much," Marilyn said. "But Daddy made up for it. At least with me."

"I showed no favoritism with any of my children." Richie stretched lazily and walked over to stand before Janet. "I'm tired. May I be excused?"

Janet smiled up at him. "You may, dear. I'll join you presently."

He turned to me. "Is there anything I can do for you, Sandra?"

"I think you've all done a great deal," I said. "I'm just sorry I can't remember any of this—or the twins."

Richie said, "Does this house seem completely strange?"

I nodded. "I knew where Larry's playroom was, but the contents weren't familiar."

"Don't fret about any of it—even not being able to place the twins," Richie said. He bent and gave Janet a good-night kiss.

Sid slid a hand beneath Marilyn's knees, cradling her and stood up. "We'd like to be excused also. I'm really bushed."

"Run along," Janet said. "Sandra's tired too. Doctor said she'll need lots of rest."

"I also need a book on how to handle children," I said.

Sid said, "Firmly," softening his admonition with a smile.

We said our good-nights and he left, carrying Marilyn, whose arms were around his neck. Her eyes opened just long enough to regard us with a smile, then closed. Sid kissed the top of her head, she murmured something softly, and he carried her from the room.

I felt a moment's envy as my eyes followed them. I supposed Larry and I had been that way, but nothing came to mind. At least, that's what I told myself, though it wasn't completely true. As I sat across from them, I thought of the blond young man with the discerning eyes and slow smile. The one who kept recurring in my dreams, yet whom I couldn't place. Where had I met him? Was he someone from my distant past? My former employer? Who?

Janet interrupted my musings with a question. "Now that we have a few minutes by ourselves, tell me, my dear, are you uneasy here or do you feel contented?"

"I'd be ungrateful to be otherwise than content," I replied, liking her more each minute. "Everyone's been very kind."

"Everyone but Nancy," Janet corrected. "However, you'll just have to do as we do—overlook her belligerency. She's always been that way. I suppose because Marilyn is so beautiful and has that certain quality that attracts people to her."

"You must be gratified that she and Sid are so happy."

"I am. She's never caused me concern. I only wish I could reach Nancy. She's a good person, but she's shut us out. It worries me, particularly since you don't remember her and may feel her resentment is directed at your presence here."

"I won't think that," I said. "I noticed she was annoyed at Sid, though I can see her side in that instance."

"Yes," Janet agreed with a shudder. "I hate killing of any kind. And how anyone who has once looked into the eyes of a deer, can raise a gun, aim, and fire, is beyond me. Yet I wouldn't censure Sid for it either."

"I don't think Marilyn would let you. It's obvious she adores him."

Janet nodded. "They're a well-matched couple and do present a striking appearance together. But enough of them. My interest just now concerns you. Is there anything special you would like to do tomorrow?"

"Yes," I replied, pleased at her question. "I'd like to shop for gifts for three of the nurses and two attendants who were very kind to me."

"You haven't changed, Sandra dear," she said. "You were always a very thoughtful person."

"Was I really?" I asked.

I must have sounded doubtful, for Janet looked puzzled.

"What is it, Sandra?"

"Nancy told me I said very unkind things to her. It sickens me to think I'd be so rude."

"Please don't brood," Janet said, "particularly about anything Nancy says. She has an overactive imagination."

"But to have told her she has no more appeal than an oil well."

Janet smiled at my perturbation. "That came out of her head. And it's not a very good comparison. A gusher has a tremendous appeal. And you're the owner of several."

"Nonetheless, I know what she means and I can understand her agony."

"But I'll swear you never made such a statement," Janet protested. "She was always coming to me with stories of Marilyn's meanness when she was a child. At first, I punished Marilyn, believing her guilty. But one time I eavesdropped on the girls. They were getting along splendidly. I was determined to find out if Marilyn was really that vicious. Satisfied, I left them. Not two minutes later Nancy sought me out in my room and embroidered such a story of sadism regarding Marilyn's treatment of her, I knew it had to be a lie. I summoned Marilyn to my room, made them both sit down and I repeated everything that had happened between them that afternoon. It so happened they were putting together a jigsaw puzzle, a very large one which took a great deal of time. At the same time, they were engaged in making light talk—girl talk

45

concerning their school, their teachers, their gym classes."

I was relieved at the revelation and to know Nancy had lied regarding my treatment of her. Her hostility was sad to behold, but it was also dangerous and I could well understand Janet's concern.

"Has she ever had therapy?" I asked.

"She's refused. And even in the little you've seen of her today, you know she couldn't be coerced into doing anything she had no interest in doing."

"And psychotherapy under protest would do no good."

"So promise me, my dear, you'll not let Nancy's accusations or petty meannesses disturb you. It will only serve to hinder your recovery."

"I promise," I said.

Janet touched her cheek to mine. "Now run along. I know you're exhausted, even though you managed a brief nap. Tomorrow you start your second life."

I arose slowly and looked around the room. At the luxurious and expensive furnishings, a silver screen at one end of the room, with filigree trim. Vases and lamps, unique and beautiful, must have been collected from the far corners of the earth. "You know, Janet, I wonder if I will ever be able to adjust to this way of life."

She looked up, her brow furrowed.

"I can't believe I ever lived in the midst of such luxury. It seems completely alien to me."

Her bewilderment evaporated in soft laughter. "From your manner, one would never know it's strange—and of course it isn't. But I'm sure you'll like it as time goes on. If you don't, you'll be an exception."

"And stupid." I joined in her laughter, then walked slowly from the room.

The bed had been turned down, a ruffled crepe nightie lay across it, and everything was ready for my bath. Relaxing in the hot, scented water, I kept my mind as empty as possible, though it wasn't easy. So much had happened to me in a single day that I could scarcely cope with it and remain calm.

I was exhausted, more than glad to get into bed. I switched off the bed lamp immediately and settled myself for sleep. I still couldn't believe it and feared I'd waken and find myself in my hospital room, with all that had

46

happened a product of my imagination or another dream.

And once again, that face materialized in my dreams. The man whose face was the only one that I seemed to remember from my past. At least, I told myself he must have been in my former life, yet I couldn't place him. I must have been in a reclining position in my dream, for it seemed as if he was bent over me, his eyes studying me seriously. Then, slowly, his mouth widened in a smile and I felt comforted.

I came awake as his face faded and I tried, as before, to place him. I wondered if Janet or Marilyn might know him and could solve the puzzle of his identity, but I hesitated to mention him because of Larry.

Fatigue soon overcame my wonderings and I slipped back into sleep, this time dreamless until awakened by sunlight shining into my face. I'd neglected to draw the draperies, but I didn't mind. I wanted to get an early start. I felt the sooner I resumed a normal life, the more apt was I to regain my memory.

At least, I thought with quiet satisfaction, I recalled yesterday from the moment I arrived at the mansion until I came upstairs to retire. No memory lapse was manifest there. I also made my mind dwell on each member of the household and the servants. I remembered them all and I had mental pictures of each of them, yet the sharpest and most familiar face was that of the blond young man from somewhere out of my past. I felt certain of that now, and I believed that if I could identify him, I might be on the road to remembering my life before the accident.

SIX

I dressed hastily, eager for the day's expedition. Before going down to breakfast, I went to the twins' room, eager to see their faces light up in a smile at sight of me. I chided myself for being so vain and foolish, then told myself it was my mother instinct.

A cry of dismay escaped me when I discovered both their rooms empty and their beds made up. I looked at Janet's door, headed for it, then turned abruptly for the stairway. She might still be deep in sleep. Downstairs, I went to the dining room. Dicie, plump and short, with fiery red hair, apple round cheeks and a cheerful smile, greeted me.

"The twins, Dicie," I said. "They're not upstairs. Are they playing outside?"

"No, Miss Sandra," she replied. "Ava took them to one of those fancy schools the little ones go to who are too young to go to regular school."

"I'm sorry I missed them."

"So am I, Miss Sandra," she replied. "Guess you'll have to get up a little earlier."

"I certainly will," I replied. "I want to be with them whenever possible."

"A good idea. They might help you to remember."

"Where is everybody?"

"Well, Mr. Sidney is an early riser. He's eaten and was at his work in the library before seven. Miss Marilyn doesn't get up until ten and Miss Nancy breakfasts around eight. Sometimes she takes things from the kitchen and cooks her own breakfast in the laboratory. Mr. Richie is off playing golf somewhere. Now may I bring your breakfast?"

"Please, but not too much."

"You're too thin, Miss Sandra, you should eat." She drew out a chair for me. "Right here, Miss."

The white cloth of the night before had been removed and breakfast, served on Madeira luncheon cloths, consisted of fresh orange juice, a mushroom omelet, hot rolls, marmalade and coffee. I apologized for not being able to finish my omelet, but complimented her on its lightness.

"Ethel supervises," she told me. "And strict she is, but I'm learnin' well here."

"Haven't you been here long?"

"Less than a month," she said. "I've only been in this country six months, not that you wouldn't know from my Irish accent."

"It's charming. And so are you, Dicie."

"Thank you, Miss. Would you like more coffee?"

"No, thank you. I'm most anxious to get going."

Ethel came from the kitchen then, carrying a tray laden with someone's breakfast. She greeted me courteously, apologizing for not being able to stop, but she was bringing Miss Janet's breakfast to her.

"Please let me," I said. "I want to talk to her."

"I'll carry it up the stairs, Miss Sandra," she said, not pausing. "I'll show you where her room is."

"I know where it is," I said, falling into step with her.

She stopped suddenly. "You *know*?" Her eyes revealed her astonishment.

"Yes. I almost stopped by before I came down to breakfast."

"Then Miss Janet told you which suite was hers," Ethel,

49

apparently satisfied she'd solved that puzzle, continued on her way.

"No, she didn't," I said quietly, hiding my joy. For the first time I realized, without being told, I knew which door was Janet's.

"Then I better stay with you once upstairs to make sure you go to the right room. Not that it would prove any embarrassment since the gentlemen have been up for some time."

At the top of the landing she paused and let me precede her. Without the slightest hesitation, I moved along the corridor to a door at the end of the wing and on the opposite side from mine. I paused and turned back to observe Ethel, a look akin almost to fear in her eyes.

"Did you see Miss Janet go in her door?" she asked.

"No," I replied. "I'm really pleased. It may be my memory loss is not as complete as I feared."

"I hope not, Miss Sandra." Her voice was barely audible and I heard the dishes rattle on the tray.

Confused by her reaction, I went back and retrieved the tray. "I'll bring it to Miss Janet."

She nodded, seeming too frightened to speak. Did she think because I had lost my memory I was a dangerous lunatic? I set the tray on the table outside the door and knocked lightly, turning back to see Ethel still standing there. I smiled reassurance and at Janet's bid to enter, I opened the door, picked up the tray and went into her room, using my hip to close the door after me.

"Sandra dear, why did you bring my tray?"

I smiled. "I asked to bring it to you, though Ethel carried it upstairs. She didn't think I knew which door was yours, but I did and she seems terrorized because of it. Is she superstitious?"

Janet laughed. "I haven't the faintest idea. But I must confess I'm astounded, unless you saw me enter or leave these rooms."

"I didn't, but just as I remembered Larry's playroom, I knew this was your suite."

"Wonderful," she exclaimed happily. "Won't Dr. Beardsley be embarrassed when we tell him your memory loss isn't total."

"Do you think he'll be more embarrassed than pleased?"

"Let's hope not. Though some doctors are so sensitive they're worse than prima donnas."

"I know, though I shouldn't speak this way. I was treated wonderfully while I was in the hospital."

"I'm glad to know that. I feel very guilty you were there so long before we found you, and then it was like pulling teeth to get Dr. Beardsley to let me see you. Are you still going out to buy gifts?"

"Yes. That's what I wanted to ask you about. Do I drive a car?"

"You do, but—and it's a big but—your wallet was never recovered and your credit cards and driving license must have been in it. Which brings us to reason number two—there's no hurry for you to get another because Dr. Beardsley said absolutely no driving. Something about stress, and there's a great deal of it in today's traffic."

I was disappointed. "Then I'll have to rely on Gilbert."

"For the present. If he's not available at any time, someone else will drive you, but he's free this morning. He's also waiting for you."

"I'll run along then. Please don't worry about me. I want to take my time and observe the town and the stores. I'm sure you know why."

Janet nodded. "Gilbert is very dependable and he'll keep an eye on you."

"Not too close a one, I hope. I must feel I'm on my own."

"We want you to and so does Dr. Beardsley. Have a good day. If you should come back for lunch, it's an impromptu sort of thing. I skip it, as does Marilyn, who watches her weight closely. Richie is never here and Sidney has a tray brought to the library. Nancy seems to get nourishment looking at her bugs. No, I'm only joking. She has a refrigerator in her lab and keeps a small supply of food there. She prefers it that way and we don't protest."

She turned to her breakfast then and I went back to my room. I'd chosen a pink silk and wool jersey. The skirt, though full, was bias cut and outlined my figure with a flattering softness with each step I took. I wished I could remember having purchased it.

The phone in my bedroom had a dial system to reach the library, kitchen, garage, and Nancy's lab. I called the

51

garage and told Gilbert I would be there shortly. I had no idea where it was, though the drive would serve as a guide. He offered to bring the car to the front, but I had a sudden desire to pay Nancy a visit before I set off on my shopping expedition. I was curious about why she'd made up such a story about me. After talking with Janet last night, I was certain she had. However, I hadn't the faintest idea of where the lab was located, but I was eager to begin a search. Such lavish and beautifully decorated grounds would be a joy to explore.

However, I'd no sooner started out when I came upon one of the gardeners, in his forest green uniform, engaged in trimming a bush. Though I'd seen the two men only briefly, I remembered the short one was named Tom. He doffed his cap as he greeted me.

"Good morning, Tom. How beautifully you keep up the grounds."

He smiled. "I can't take credit for it, Miss, since I've only been here two months."

"Where is the laboratory? As you've probably been told, I suffered a loss of memory in the accident."

"Yes, Miss. Just follow that path beneath the rose arbors and you'll come to it."

"Thank you," I said. I followed the path and discovered the laboratory was a one-room, shed-like affair with windows curtained though they'd been pushed aside to let in as much daylight as possible. Two high-backed rockers set in the center of the room.

Within, I discovered Nancy in a stained gray smock, bent over a binocular microscope. There were three others on the long bench and an assortment of weird-looking apparatus. Chemicals and more apparatus crowded the several shelves. The place was neat and orderly, the equipment clean, denoting fastidious care.

"Hello, Nancy."

She looked up, startled at my appearance, then said, "Hi, Sandy."

"I was curious to see what your lab looked like and decided to stop by before I went shopping."

"Thanks." She seemed uncertain I was speaking the truth. "Did Mother know you were coming here?"

"No. It was a spontaneous thing on my part."

She was silent a moment, digesting what I said. "Well, thanks for coming. No one else ever does. Marilyn says the stink makes her ill."

"I don't smell anything," I said.

"Of course you don't. She imagines it. The protozoans frighten her. She thinks they're disease germs and she'll catch something."

"It's quite a lab," I said. "I used to go down to the pathology department of the hospital and it wasn't as well equipped as this seems to be."

"I spent too much on it, I know. But Larry indulged me. He knew it was all I had to keep my interests alive. What I'm trying to do is prepare a series of slides showing every facet of the life of these animals. They are animals, you know. Much bigger than bacteria, of course. In fact, they feed on germs."

"I'm headed for town," I explained, "but one day soon I'd like you to show me what this is all about. I truly respect science, Nancy. I'm all for anyone who devotes time to it."

She seemed too astounded to reply.

"Don't you believe me?"

Her mouth twisted in what was apparently meant to be a smile, though it could have been a sneer. "It's kind of hard to when you never came here before. In fact, you used to call me . . ."

"Please don't tell me," I broke in before she could finish the sentence. It was probably another of her lies, though I'd not let her know Janet had told me of the antagonism Nancy bore the family. "I want to change. Or perhaps I have changed. Maybe the accident did some good. The fact is, I want you to like me, Nancy. Please give me a second chance."

She still didn't look convinced, but the tenseness around her mouth softened. "You don't have to ask a favor like that of me. I'm not a monster."

"I know that. You're a scientist, Nancy. I've been exposed to a great deal of it since my accident. I quite likely owe my life to it."

"That would account for your interest, certainly. If you wish to come here any time and are really interested, okay."

I thanked her and left, hopeful I'd made a little progress in changing her attitude toward me. I went to the garage and looked over the cars.

I found a fireman red Porsche, a diamond blue Cadillac, a black Fiat racer—or it looked much like one. There was a rakish-looking station wagon, a T-bird, a small utility truck and a rack of bicycles. Gilbert approached me.

"Good heavens," I said, "it looks like a Hertz parking lot."

"All members of the family drive, ma'am," Gilbert said. "Sometimes all the cars are out at one time. It's a busy garage."

"I'm sure of it. Whose car is whose, Gilbert?"

His seamed face took on a pleased look. "They are really yours, ma'am."

"Aren't the cars assigned to any particular person?"

"No, ma'am. Miss Marilyn and Miss Nancy fight over the Porsche quite often."

"Do I drive, Gilbert?"

"Yes, ma'am. Very well too, if I may say so."

"I'm glad to hear that."

"But doctor's orders are you can't drive for awhile yet."

"I know. I want to go to a shopping area to buy some gifts for my friends at the hospital. I'm not quite sure just where. . . ."

"I know, ma'am. Leave it to me."

"Thank you, Gilbert. I will."

I got into the car, feeling a trifle foolish in the back seat. It seemed to me I should be accustomed to this but I was not. Then I thought of something else as the car sped along Sunset Boulevard.

"Gilbert." I tapped on the window separating us. It slid back, operated by some control he managed. "Gilbert, I haven't any money with me. Not a cent. It slipped my mind to ask about this. Do you know where I bank?"

"Yes ma'am . . . the main bank, that is. Shall I take you there?"

"Please," I said. If I was wealthy enough for all the luxury that surrounded me, it was time I began to take on some responsibilities.

He turned down a side street and we emerged in Beverly

Hills. He pulled up in a no-parking area in front of an imposing-looking bank. He got out and held the door open for me.

"Ask for Mr. Oleander, ma'am, in case you've forgotten."

"Thank you. I have indeed forgotten."

I entered the bank and, so far as I knew, I'd never been here before. It was large and very busy. Every desk at which officials sat was busy. I approached a uniformed security officer and asked for Mr. Oleander. He pointed in the direction of the largest and nearest desk in the lobby. It bore Mr. Oleander's name and his title of manager. I approached the desk. A young girl, neatly attired in skirt and blouse, looked up from her smaller desk.

"You'll have to wait," she said.

"I'm only looking for information. Perhaps you can help me."

"Sit down and wait, Miss," she instructed me.

"Very well, if I must. Please tell Mr. Oleander that Mrs. Larrabee. . . ."

The girl's mouth was already agape. She eyed me with new interest, excused herself, hurried to the big desk and whispered in Mr. Oleander's ear. He arose, regarded me with surprise, but gave me a warm smile. He spoke to the two people with whom he'd been conferring and whatever he told them, they promptly withdrew to take chairs in the waiting section of the lobby. Mr. Oleander came toward me with his hand outstretched. He was a middle-aged, neatly dressed man with a self-assured manner, indicative of his skill in dealing with clients.

"Mrs. Larrabee! What a pleasant surprise. It's good to see you again."

"Thank you, Mr. Oleander." I sat down beside his desk. I noticed that the occupants of desks close by had ceased work and the officials were regarding me with ill-concealed astonishment.

"I find that I came away without any money," I said. "Please bear with me because I've lost my memory as the result of an accident and some of the things I say may sound absurd. Do I have an account here?"

"Certainly, Mrs. Larrabee." Mr. Oleander's tone was

55

sympathetic. "I'm sorry about your accident, but I'm glad you're with us again. And you look well."

"Thank you," I said.

"I presume you came to make a withdrawal."

"Yes, please."

"You may have anything up to a million. With a little time, we could make it five million. Just tell me how much you wish and I'll verify it with Mr. Burwell."

"May I ask why it needs to be verified?"

"Mr. Burwell handles the financial details of the Larrabee estate. It relieves you of responsibility and I must say he does a marvelous job. Just a moment, please." He picked up his phone. "Get me Mr. Burwell, please." He glanced at me. "How much will you require, Mrs. Larrabee?"

I was about to ask for fifty dollars, but I had an idea that wouldn't be quite in keeping with my wealth. "Five hundred will be sufficient," I said.

He turned his attention to the phone. "Mr. Burwell, Oleander here. Mrs. Larrabee is in the bank with a request for cash. In any amount. Yes, of course. Thank you, sir." He hung up, pressed a button under his desk and dispatched a page girl for the money. It was counted out before me in two minutes.

"Don't I have to sign?" I asked.

"No. Mr. Burwell will issue a check on your account. It's indeed a pleasure to see you again and to serve you."

I tucked the five hundred into the handbag I'd taken from a closet cabinet full of them and thought this wasn't a bad life after all. I could have asked for fifty thousand and had it in my hands promptly. The thought amused me, for I wondered what I'd have done with it.

Gilbert brought me to one of the luxury department stores on Wilshire Boulevard. I had another thought. "Gilbert, do we have charge accounts here?"

"Ma'am, there isn't a store in Los Angeles or Beverly Hills that won't honor your request for credit. You have but to ask."

"Well, I may try it. If I run into trouble, I'll call on you for identification."

"I'll be waiting," he said dutifully. "But I'm sure they'll recognize you."

I entered the store, browsed through the different departments without being approached by any clerks. I stopped at a counter that sold hosiery. I ordered three dozen, to be boxed half a dozen each. The clerk pondered that order.

"Will it be a charge, madam?"

"Yes. I'm Mrs. Larry Larrabee."

In the twinkling of an eye, another clerk was at my side and a customer's relations woman was guiding me about, suggesting things after I explained I wanted gifts for hospital people. A carry-boy lugged the stack of boxes out to where the car waited. I signed a charge slip and joined my purchases in the car.

I stayed at the hospital for two hours, thanking everyone who had been involved with my recovery. It was fun rewarding them. Like coming home. Not to that Sunset Boulevard mansion, but the only home I'd known before that. I even visited my old room for a few moments and sympathized with the new patient who was to undergo surgery next morning.

It occurred to me that I'd forgotten the person who had done the most for me. Dr. Beardsley! He deserved the best possible gift I could find. Gilbert waited beside the car. Before I got into the car, I said, "Is there a Robertson Boulevard, Gilbert?"

"Yes, Miss Sandra."

"Do you know if I went there before my accident?"

"I don't know, because you always drove. I'm sorry."

"It's all right, Gilbert. For some reason I wish to go there to make a purchase. It seems as if I'll find what I want there."

He regarded me with wonder. "You mean you know the name of a shop you want me to take you to?"

"No. But I have a feeling it's on that street."

"I hope so, Miss. There are a number of fashionable shops in that area. You probably went there often."

"Take me there and cruise the street, please."

Robertson proved to be in Beverly Hills and, as Gilbert had stated, there were many exclusive shops along this street. I knew Dr. Beardsley was an avid collector of Grecian artifacts, and when I saw a small store devoted to such items, I had Gilbert pull over. He had to drive a block beyond the establishment before he found a slot to pull into. He helped me out and deposited a coin in the meter.

"Sure you'll be all right, Miss Sandra?"

"Quite sure, Gilbert, though I may be a while."

I walked down the street, looking in windows, thoroughly enjoying myself. I felt like someone out of prison and reveling in my freedom, I was also quite intrigued by the fact that I could buy anything I wished. It was an odd sensation and it seemed strange and unique.

I found myself looking into a basement book store. Not the ordinary kind, but one dealing in rare volumes. Leather-bound tomes. The entire store looked bound in leather. I sensed that I'd been here before. I would have sworn I had.

I walked down the four cement steps, pushed open the door and I knew a small bell above it would ring and bring the proprietor out from a back room. Sure enough, there was such a bell and when a man, no more than five feet tall, shuffled out from the rear of the store, I felt certain I'd not only seen him before, but had had dealings with him.

"Good afternoon, Miss," he said, his bow courtly. His eyes looked enormous behind thick lenses set in a heavy black frame.

"Good afternoon. I'm not certain I'm in the right store. I thought I'd been here before. Do you know me? Have you seen me before?"

His magnified eyes scanned my face. He shook his head. "Sorry, Miss."

My high spirits deflated. "I was so sure I'd been here several times."

"I don't remember you. Is there a book you asked me about? A rare volume, perhaps, that you wanted to purchase?"

Behind me I heard the little bell tinkle again and the proprietor looked up, but didn't evidence any interest. Someone was moving about behind me. I paid no heed, too intent on my own disappointment.

"I'm afraid not," I said. "Thank you very much. I know now that I must have been mistaken."

I turned to leave and came to a dead stop. I thought

58

my heart had done the same thing. I felt the blood drain out of my face and I stood there, speechless.

I was looking straight into the face I'd dreamed about so frequently. I almost spoke, but caught myself, though there was no question but that it was he. The same inquisitive gaze, the blond hair bleached by the sun, the craggy face and warm smile that was even now beginning to form. I noticed something else. His nose jutted ever so slightly to one side. I found it appealing. He was well over six feet and the shoulders were as broad as they'd been in my recurring dream. But he wasn't a figment of my unconscious mind. He was a warm human being who seemed pleased at sight of me.

"Hello," he said. His voice was deep and masculine and warm.

SEVEN

I felt confused and stupid and bewildered. I thought I was back in my bed and I'd awaken to have him dissolve with the recurring dream I'd had of him.

He said, "Is something wrong?"

"Yes . . . no . . . I'm sorry." My smile was apologetic. "I know I'm acting foolish, but for a moment you looked familiar. Have we met sometime in the past?"

His easy smile was the one I'd seen in my dreams of him. "Do you think we have?"

"I don't know. It seems as if we have, yet I must be mistaken. I'm sure I am."

"Why are you so sure?" he asked. He seemed to be countering my questions with those of his own, yet I could feel no offense.

I felt foolish. "I guess this just isn't my day. I came in this store, believing I'd been here several times before, but the proprietor can't recall ever having seen me."

"Do you have trouble with your memory?"

I nodded. "I was in an accident and suffered head injuries. I was released from the hospital only yesterday and I'm trying. . . ." I broke off, embarrassed. "Forgive me. I shouldn't be going on this way. It's just that I thought I might have known you from somewhere. Your face seems familiar."

"I'm flattered. I'd be honored to think I was considered a friend."

"Thank you. Good-bye." I finally got my wits together and ended this foolish conversation. Foolish on my part.

He stepped aside, but I was certain his eyes followed me as I left the shop. I knew beyond a doubt it was his face that haunted my dreams. Nothing about him seemed strange. Even his voice had a familiar ring to it. Yet it was all hazy—as if it had to be a dream, yet now I knew it wasn't. He was flesh and blood, as real as I.

I fought off an urge to return to the store and question him, urge him to tell me if he knew me. Somehow, I had a feeling he did, and was holding back. But why? What reason could he have for doing so? Unless he was part of my past—a part he didn't wish to admit to being. My head started to ache and I forced all thoughts of him from my mind to concentrate on my gift to Dr. Beardsley. I found what I wanted, at an exorbitant price, but the good doctor had saved my reason, had held many sessions with me, even before he knew my identity. I was greatly indebted to him and was pleased to have the statue, dug up somewhere in Greece, sent to him.

I headed back to the car and caught sight of Gilbert. He hadn't seen me and he was peering into each store window, seeking a glimpse of me, the wrinkles in his face deepened with concern.

I walked up to him. "Here I am, Gilbert."

He turned abruptly. "Oh, Miss Sandra. I was afraid something might have happened to you. Miss Janet would never forgive me."

"You shouldn't have worried. I was thoroughly enjoying myself."

"I'm glad, Miss. I thought for a minute you might have forgotten where the car was and were wandering about. I was afraid you might get careless."

I smiled. "You mean step out in the road and get struck by a car."

"Yes, Miss."

"My lack of memory doesn't make me less wary," I

61

said. "I'm probably more cautious than ever. Especially as a pedestrian."

"I know what you mean, Miss. Well, are you ready to go back to the car?"

He looked no less worried and I gathered he'd be relieved when he had me safely back to the house. However, we were no sooner on our way than I had a sudden exciting thought.

"Gilbert, please stop by to pick up the children—unless they're already at home."

"Maybe I should take you home first. Miss Janet might be annoyed with me for your being gone so long."

"She won't be," I assured him. "I told her not to worry—that I intended to take my time."

He nodded. "In that case, I can relax."

"Do, for heaven's sake. I'll not be babied. Not by you or my mother-in-law or anyone else in the family. I'm determined to regain my memory and I feel the best way to do it is to be as active as possible. That I intend to do."

"I'm glad, Miss. You're beginning to sound like your old self."

"Since I have no memory, I don't know how my old self sounded."

"Spirited, Miss. Spirited."

I smiled, wondering if he meant difficult—or rude. If Nancy spoke the truth, I had been. Janet said she'd lied and had always been in the habit of doing so. Nonetheless, I was glad I'd stopped by her laboratory this morning. I hoped I'd made a start toward a friendlier relationship there.

The school, located in Santa Monica, was set well back from the street and framed with beautifully cared for shrubbery, plus shade trees which had not yet attained their full growth. The building was modern and the play yard well-furnished with equipment to keep the children amused. There were a few children playing there now, supervised by a teacher.

Gilbert said, "I'm a little late. When that happens, the children play in the yard until they're called for."

"I didn't know you were to pick them up. I'm sorry."

"It's all right, Miss. No harm done. I was late once before."

I had the feeling I was being gently chided for interfering with his routine and keeping Christine and Carol waiting, but the routine of the household was still alien to me.

Gilbert excused himself and went to get the children. My heart warmed at the sight of them when they left the group and ran ahead of him, red coats covering dresses of a matching color. Their hair streamed behind them as they ran to the car. I opened the door and they scrambled in, giggling and exclaiming in delight at sight of me. I patted the seat on either side of me and they took their places, both looking up at me. I colored at the warmth of their gaze.

"Thanks for coming," Christine said. "It's the first time."

I laughed. "You mean since I got back."

"No," Christine said. "You never came before."

"I'm ashamed of myself. I promise to do better from now on."

I slipped an arm about each of the twins and drew them close. They snuggled against me willingly.

"Mommy, you don't smell of flowers." Carol was the serious one, the observant one.

Christine shifted herself to a kneeling position and sniffed at my hairline. "No, she doesn't."

"I'm sorry," I said. "I forgot all about putting on perfume. I'll remember from now on."

"Did you see our play yard, Mommy?" Christine was once again snuggled against me. "Grandma had it made for us while you were in the hospital."

"No, I haven't," I admitted.

"Please let us show it to you when we get home," she said. "It's beautiful. Almost as much fun as the one at school."

"I want to see it," I exclaimed.

"Of course, you can't ride on any of the things because you're too big," Carol said. "But you can watch us."

"That's what I really want to do," I told her. My arms were around them and I squeezed them gently, for greater assurance.

"We'll have to change first," Carol said. "These are

63

our school clothes. Grandma had our names written on everything so you would know us apart."

"I already know you apart," I said. "Even without your names."

"How do you know us, Mommy?" Christine asked.

"Let me think how I can best tell you." I was quiet a moment, then said, "I know. You, Christine, are like a beautiful sunrise, bright and exciting; while you, Carol, are like soft moonlight, quiet and mysterious."

"I would like to be both." Christine spoke in a very grown-up manner.

"I suppose that's the ideal of every woman," I replied. "I didn't realize a girl as little as you would know it."

"I know it, Mommy," Christine said. "That's how Aunt Marilyn is."

"That's exactly how she is," I replied, amazed at the child's discernment.

"Nancy is like a rainy day," Christine went on. "A bad rainy day."

"What do you mean—a bad rainy day?" I said. "Rainy days are fun."

"I mean a day when you've been promised a picnic and it rains and you can't have it."

"I don't see Nancy that way," I said.

"How do you see her?" Carol asked.

"I think she's very lonely," I said. "And because she's lonely, she's unhappy."

"No, she isn't," Christine disputed. "She has her bugs and that's all she cares about."

Carol said, "She showed them to me."

"How nice of her," I said.

"She told me things about them too," Carol went on. "They're good bugs. She said we have to have them in the world."

Christine said, "I step on bugs."

"I step on spiders," Carol said. "And ants. But you can't see the kind of bugs Aunt Nancy has."

"If I could, I'd step on them too," Christine said giggling. "I don't like Nancy."

"That's unkind," I said. "I want you to like everyone. If you can't, just be quiet about it."

64

Her eyes brimmed at my mild chastisement. "You weren't nice to Nancy before the accident."

"I wasn't?" Then why had Janet told me Nancy was lying about that, I wondered. Maybe Janet had just wanted to make me feel better—but still, it was unfair to Nancy.

Christine disengaged herself from my arm and leaned across my lap to address Carol. "Wasn't Mommy mean to Nancy?"

"Yes." Carol's reply was barely audible.

"Then I'm very ashamed of myself," I said. "I'll never be unkind to her again."

"Maybe you couldn't help it, Mommy," Carol said loyally. "You had awful bad headaches."

"Yes, you did," Christine said.

"Before I had the accident?" I asked.

"Yes," both girls chorused.

Had Janet lied to reassure me? Certainly the children weren't lying. Not Carol, at any rate. Christine might embroider a story, but not Carol. She was a very somber child. Though they were identical twins, their personalities were quite different.

We'd reached the house and the twins ran ahead to change into jeans and sweaters. I met Janet in the corridor on my way to my room.

"Was your outing pleasant?" she asked.

"Very," I replied.

"Did anything nudge your memory?"

I almost mentioned the man who owned the bookstore and the young man of my dreams I'd confronted there, but I refrained lest Janet think me foolish.

"It was quite uneventful except that I worried Gilbert by my prolonged absence."

She smiled. "He's like a mother hen the way he watches over the women in this family—except Nancy, of course. She'll not allow it. I marvel she hasn't joined Woman's Lib."

"Maybe she has," I said.

Janet's brows raised. "Maybe. We'd be the last to know. Anyway, we're having a welcome-home party for you this evening."

"So soon?" I exclaimed in dismay.

"Nothing elaborate." She rested a hand on my arm

in a further effort to reassure me. "We thought it might be good for you. You loved parties and they're all people who knew you. We're hoping one of them might stir your memory."

I relented. "You're right. I'll have to face them sooner or later. However, I promised the twins I'd take them out and let them show me the playground you put in for them."

"It was your idea, really. You'd promised it to them. Then you disappeared and I had it put in. I hope you don't mind."

"I'm grateful."

She started to move away, then paused to say, "Oh, Sandra, please dress for dinner."

"I will." There wasn't time to say more, for the twins came pounding down the stairs, Christine in the lead. She was the aggressive one, the extrovert. However, I sensed Carol had a mind of her own. She also was gifted with a great deal of compassion. I wondered whether she inherited it from me or—Larry. His name came into my mind hesitantly. How I wished the curtain would lift and my past would be revealed, but I had no time to dwell on it, for the girls each took one of my hands, with Christine tugging me almost into a run.

The playground was some distance from the house, beyond the laboratory and cut off from it by a grove of spruce. Indeed, it was almost as lavish as the one at the school they attended. It had several swings, seesaws, a basketball court in miniature, a ping pong table in an open-air playhouse which was roofed against rain, and there was a vast labyrinth of vari-colored cubes piled on one another and going in various directions. It was a sort of cave-like arrangement in which children could exercise their muscles by alternately climbing and crawling.

The girls performed on some of the equipment, climbed through the cubes, calling out to me to find them. I couldn't, but I called back that I had to return to the house, that there was to be a dinner party and it was getting late. They appeared miraculously, begging to be allowed to attend.

I had no idea what the protocol was, but I couldn't resist their pleas, particularly not after they told me they had party dresses which reached to their ankles, so I said they might dress up and come downstairs and mingle with the guests for a while.

Satisfied, we returned to the house. Rather, I should say I did. They ran on ahead, stating they had to tell Ava I'd given permission for them to come downstairs and they must have their baths before they dressed.

EIGHT

I took care to splash my body with eau de cologne and spray on perfume. It was readily available in oversize atomizers on my dressing table in the powder room. I liked the scent and could understand why the children liked it. It was a light floral essence, not overwhelming, and reminded me of the fresh fragrance of flowers after a rain.

I chose a long-sleeved, high-necked white chiffon floor-length gown. It was devoid of trimming, but full-skirted and billowed out with my slightest movement. I felt quite elegant in it and once again marveled that I'd been accustomed to this.

I went to the jewelry chest and opened the narrow top drawer. I selected a pair of drop pearl earrings from among the many sets nestled in their satin bed.

I was giving myself a final appraisal in the mirror when I heard a soft knock on my door, followed by Marilyn's request to enter. I called out an assent and when we met in the sitting room, she exclaimed with delight at sight of me. As for me, I was overwhelmed by her beauty. I could readily see why Janet and Richie had christened her their golden girl.

Everything about her was so perfect and so beautiful and her pale green gown accented that beauty.

She said, "Despite the fact that you've lost weight, your gown fits perfectly."

"I can't imagine ever having worn anything so beautiful before," I said.

"You did," she assured me. "But not that. Larry loved to see you dressed up and during his illness you went on a buying spree and kept yourself looking very alluring. Even in the final days of his illness, his eyes brightened whenever you entered the room. However, several gowns, dresses, and outfits you never had on because his tragic death was mercifully swift."

"Then that's why my wardrobe seems so new," I said.

"That's why," she repeated. "I understand you're bringing the twins downstairs."

"They begged me to," I said. "I felt it harmless and, to them, exciting."

"Exactly," Marilyn agreed. "Mother's pleasantly surprised."

"Why?"

She lowered her eyes. "No reason."

"I think there is a reason," I said. "Please be honest with me. At all times. I'm trying desperately to go back into the past. To find myself and bridge my past with my present. I want to know everything about myself."

"Well," Marilyn began hesitantly, "perhaps you should know, though Mother cautioned me to say nothing that would upset you."

"I'll be far more upset wondering what it is you're keeping from me."

"I agree. The fact is, you never bothered much with the twins. Mother worried about it, Nancy despised you because of it. I felt that once Larry was gone, you would change."

"But I didn't."

"Well, of course, you were pretty upset. But when their birthday approached, you agreed to come with me and help choose new dresses for them. It was the first time you went out with any of us since Larry's death. Unfortunately, you slipped away from me. The rest you know."

"You mean the accident," I said.

She nodded.

I felt ashamed of myself. "Maybe the accident did more good than harm."

"You've changed," Marilyn admitted. "But please don't dwell on the way you were before. We're so happy to have you back and only hope you're as happy to be back."

"I am," I said. "Yet I feel like Cinderella."

"Why should you," Marilyn said with a smile, "when everything in this house is yours? When each member of the family is completely dependent on your largess."

I pressed my fingertips against my temples in a vain attempt to remember. It seemed too much to accept—the fact that I was an heiress. I could think of no other word.

"Anyway," Marilyn went on, "Ava has the twins ready and they're impatient for you to come for them. Now do you mind if I go downstairs with Mother and help her greet the guests who should be arriving momentarily? There'll be cocktails and dancing before dinner. The ballroom is situated at the rear of the house. I don't think you've seen it, but the music will draw you there. Don't be nervous or frightened. You know everybody who'll be there—even though some only casually."

"But will I remember them?" I suddenly felt panicky.

"We hope so. That's why Mother is giving the affair. It was a spur-of-the-moment thing. She hopes someone or something will raise the curtain on your life before the accident."

"So do I," I said. "I'll thank Janet when I see her."

"Just don't be frightened," Marilyn called from the door. I walked over to the window and watched the cars already moving up the drive and prayed silently that among the guests would be one to jog my memory. I turned then and walked out of the suite.

Sid met me in the hall, carrying two oversize glasses filled with a colorless liquid. He offered me one. "Vodka martinis. Your favorite."

"No, thanks," I said.

"Won't you drink with me any more? Not even a toast to the future?"

He looked so dismayed, I relented. "Very well. I'll

70

take a sip. No more though. This is going to be quite an ordeal for me."

"It's been a long time," he admitted. "But you'll weather it beautifully."

"I hope so."

He handed me the glass. "Here's to a complete recovery."

"Thanks, Sid." We touched glasses.

He said, "I came up to tell you your jewelry—the good stuff—is in the safe in the library. Would you like to wear some?"

"No." I touched my pearl earrings. "These will do."

"That's costume stuff. Your genuine pearls are downstairs."

"These suit me fine."

"Also your best wristwatch."

"Somehow I'm not excited even at the thought of looking at it," I said.

"That doesn't sound like you." Sid half emptied his glass in three swallows. "You worshipped the real stuff, but you had sense enough to know you couldn't wear it outside. Not much sense in having it anymore. Even tonight, we've hired private detectives to mingle among the guests to make certain no party crasher will make a haul. Also, we have sentry dogs and watchmen on the premises at all times. The gate is electrically controlled and the fence is high enough to discourage any but confirmed athletes. Or someone provided with a grappling hook and rope ladder. Don't you like your drink?"

I set it on the table, not having taken more than the one sip from it. "I'm bringing the children downstairs. I promised them."

Sid looked surprised. "You are?"

I smiled. "I think it's about time I realized my responsibilities as a mother."

He looked regretful. "Good for you, Sandy, but I guess it means I lose a drinking companion."

His statement startled me. "Was I an alcoholic?"

"Certainly not. We were social drinkers."

"You mean you were." I bit at my lower lip.

"Larry's death hit you hard," he replied. "So you took to the bottle. Not here. You'd go away. Sometimes you'd

71

call us to come for you. Other times you returned yourself. We worried like hell over you."

I lowered my eyes, suddenly hating myself, wondering where I'd gone, what I'd done and if I'd sought out other drinking companions.

Sid finished his drink, set down his glass, and gripped my arm lightly. "I thought you'd been told, Sandy. Otherwise, I'd never have mentioned it."

"I'm glad you did," I said. "I want to know me as I was. Certainly I'll do everything not to revert. Only, all of a sudden, I'm frightened at what I'll see when the curtain on my mind lifts."

"It wasn't that bad," he disputed. "So don't start getting guilt feelings. Oh—one more thing. Your diamond wedding ring and engagement ring were missing. Your credit cards were stolen when your handbag was swiped. We put a stop on them. No one ever tried to use them, so obviously the thief threw them away. Do you want me to see to it you get new ones?"

"Not immediately," I said. "I can get whatever cash I want."

"You certainly can. All you need do is step into the bank for any amount you wish."

"Don't I have to sign?"

"I do that. And don't try to cash a check in your name. The account is in the name of the estate. But you may have any amount you wish."

"I know. Mr. Oleander mentioned five million."

"Much more than that, Sandy. We'll go over the books whenever you like. Of course, you can always draw on the estate and set up your own checking account."

"Not yet, Sidney. I'd prefer you continue to handle things for the present."

He looked pleased. "Thanks, Sandy. Now run along and get the twins. I wondered what they were squealing about when I passed their door."

I nodded and moved down the corridor. As I turned into their room, I noticed Sid pick up my glass, take a deep swallow and head for the stairs.

I entered the twins' room. Instead of rushing over to me, they stood, awaiting my approval. They were enchanting in their long dresses, with empire waistlines and wide sash tied in a bow at the back with ends touching the hem of their dresses. Ava stood alongside them, her face widened in a smile.

I said, "How beautiful you both look." I knelt on one knee and extended my arms to them. They rushed to me, their smiles ecstatic. Their arms went around my neck and they kissed my cheeks. I returned their kiss and embrace.

Christine said, "Thanks for letting us come to the party."

I said, "I'll be very proud going downstairs with you."

Carol said, "You look beautiful, Mommy. And you smell like you used to."

I kissed the tip of her nose. "I put it on just for you. Both of you," I amended, telling myself I must never seem to favor one over the other.

I straightened and took each by the hand. I dreaded the moment of having to face the guests, but I could delay it no longer. Already, the strains of the orchestra drifted up the stairwell, filtering through the hall. I complimented Ava on the twins' appearance and we left the nursery.

The three of us paused at the landing and looked down into the reception hall which was now well filled with beautifully gowned ladies and their male escorts. Jewels glittered in the light from the chandeliers and the fragrance of expensive perfumes filled the air.

Carol and Christine were genuinely awed, but not to the point of speechlessness. They exclaimed in delight at the scene below and pulled at my hands in their eagerness to be a part of it. As we descended, as if in an unspoken signal, I felt fifty pair of eyes regarding us. Some revealed curiosity, some surprise (perhaps at sight of me with the twins), some even looked pleased.

I moved about them, still with the twins who responded politely when they were spoken to. I had no idea who these people were, yet they were quite at ease with me. I nodded a greeting, thanked them when they told me how well I looked and how pleased they were at my recovery. None of them asked questions of me and I surmised they were told beforehand just to accept me. They did—and graciously.

I moved gradually to the rear of the hall and the

entrance to the ballroom. A four-piece combo played softly, a fact which gratified me. The conversations had resumed and the jumble of words irritated me. I suppose because I was beginning to feel fatigue. I appreciated Janet's good intentions, but my common sense told me I wasn't ready for this sort of thing.

As if I'd voiced what was in my mind, Janet came up to me. "Are you tired, dear?"

"A little," I admitted.

"I suppose I was premature, but when you said you were going to do everything possible in an effort to regain your memory, I thought I'd do my part. Let me take the twins off your hands."

"Oh no," I protested.

"Oh yes," she said. "You can't mix with them hanging on to you. I'll see that they have a good time."

I looked down at them. "Would you mind, darlings?"

"No, Mommy, so long as we can stay."

"For an hour," I said. "Will you mind, Janet?"

"Not a bit. After cocktails, we're having dinner. Do have a drink, dear. It will relax you."

"I'd rather not," I said. "I understand I. . . ."

I didn't need to finish. Janet's face flushed angrily. "Who told you?"

"Sid thought I'd been told," I said.

"I'm sorry," she said. "That's one thing I felt shouldn't be mentioned."

"I'm glad I know," I said. "I'll make certain it doesn't happen from now on. But until I'm sure of myself, I'll avoid alcohol." She looked pleased. Perhaps reassured would be a better word. I touched my cheek to hers, adding, "So please don't worry about me."

"I can see I have no reason to." She moved away then, with the twins in tow.

Ethel, in black with white touches at her throat, was moving unobtrusively about. She saw me and came up to greet me. "I hope everything meets with your approval, Miss Sandra."

"It's a lovely party. You're to be commended."

"It's catered, of course. But I see that everything is going as I know you'd wish it to."

"Thank you, Ethel."

She smiled and moved away.

Behind me, a man spoke in a soft voice. "Good evening, Mrs. Larrabee. May I have this dance?"

I knew who it was as I turned. I faced the man in the bookstore, the man who dominated my dreams, the only person who I sensed I'd known, yet couldn't place. I was too surprised to acknowledge his greeting, but I didn't protest when his arm went about my waist and he drew me onto the dance floor. Our bodies moved in unison to the music and our eyes bore an intimacy that was almost embarrassing. My heart was beating much too fast and I felt the thumb of his left hand against my pulse. He must know the devastating effect he was having on me. I had to discipline myself before anyone else noticed.

However, I was determined to learn who he was before the evening was over. Certainly he was playing a little game with me. Why had he been so evasive at the bookstore? Either he was a friend of the family, or he'd known me before the accident. And if it was the latter, how had he got here? It was time I found out.

NINE

He was studying my face with an intentness I found embarrassing. I'd been observed that way in the hospital by doctors who would come in to check on me. But certainly he was no part of that.

"The scars," he said, "barely show."

"Scars?" I asked.

"The ones at the hairline where they repaired some of the damage to your face. It's a superlative job of plastic surgery."

"Who are you?" A trace of irritation tinged my voice.

"Please don't be angry with me."

"I don't like riddles," I said. "Especially now when my life seems to be one. You must be a guest, so why be mysterious? I'll even overlook the incident at the bookstore when you pretended not to know me."

"I don't really know you, Mrs. Larrabee," he said. "But I was hoping you remembered me."

"Then you know the family."

"No." His features relaxed as a smile touched his mouth. "I crashed the party. It's no problem in Los Angeles. All one needs is a tuxedo and a lot of cheek.

Then you greet the guard at the gate as if you're an old friend of the family. Of course, I borrowed a Porsche to make it seem more as if I belonged to this crowd."

"Don't you?"

"No."

"I should order you off the premises, but I won't."

"Why not?" His eyes were mocking me.

"Not because I find you irresistible, but I happen to have a woman's curiosity and I'm anxious to know why you denied knowing me in that bookstore."

"Is that the first time you remember seeing me?"

I hesitated a moment, then said, "Yes." I couldn't tell him about the recurring dream in which he seemed to be bent over and looking down at me. I'd sound stupid.

"Suppose we take a stroll outside. Too many people around here."

"Very well." I kept my manner casual, though my heart seemed to be beating at twice its normal rate. "First, I must speak to my mother-in-law about a place at one of the tables for you."

"Next to you," he said.

I had to smile. "You're not exactly shy, are you?"

"I can't afford to be. Whether you know it or not, we have a lot to discuss."

"In that case, don't you think it would be wise for me to know your name? My mother-in-law watches over me like a mother hen and I doubt she'd appreciate a party crasher unless he had a specific reason for coming here."

"The name is Douglas Lansing. Please refer to me as Doug when you speak to her. I mean—pretend we've been friends."

"How can I, when I don't know if we've ever met?"

"We've met," he assured me.

"In the bookstore this afternoon?"

"Before that."

"Yet you denied it."

"I told you I wanted to see if you remembered me."

"Tell me—did I meet you before the accident?"

"No."

"In the hospital?"

"Yes."

"Then why can't I remember you?"

"That's what I want to talk to you about," he said. "Oh, just say you met me this afternoon and invited me here this evening."

My eyes mocked him. "For a casual evening. Yet you came in a tuxedo."

He smiled. "Maybe you don't remember your past, but you have a keen mind. About the tux, I saw a notice in the morning paper that Mrs. Larrabee was giving a small dinner," he accented the *small* with a wry look, "to celebrate the return of her daughter-in-law from the hospital."

I excused myself and found Janet engaged in conversation with a group. I asked to speak to her and we moved beyond the hearing of those around us.

"There's a gentleman here whom I met in the hospital. He saw the notice in the paper of the dinner tonight and came. I hope you don't mind."

"Not a bit," she assured me. "I'll place him at your table. We've set up tables with place settings for six in the drawing room. I had you with two elderly couples and Nancy. I'll put Nancy elsewhere."

"Please don't," I said. "She may be hurt."

Janet gave my arm a reassuring pat. "She'll get over it."

"No." I was firm. "I want her at the table. I want to win her friendship and I'm sure Doug won't mind."

"Why didn't you tell me about him?"

"I forgot." For one who didn't practice guile, I was doing well. Or was I adept at the art? I didn't know.

"Well, run along, dear. I'm sure we can get an extra setting at the table."

I made my way among the guests to the door where I glimpsed Douglas Lansing. He seemed to tower above the others and as he watched me approach, I noted a softness to his eyes that warmed me. I was eager to be with him —the man of my dreams who I now knew wasn't really part of my dream world, but a flesh-and-blood being.

Just before we stepped out into the darkness, I caught a glimpse of Janet standing at the entrance to the drawing room. She too was curious as to who Douglas Lansing was and had waited to see whom I would return to. I couldn't help but smile at the surprise still registered on her face, though hers was no greater than mine.

Fortunately, the night was balmy—one of those rare evenings that are like a warm summer night back East. We moved away from the house, keeping to a stone walk, our way lighted by a beautiful full moon.

"Tell me now," he said, "where did we meet?"

"I don't know," I replied.

"Then what makes you think you know me?"

"I don't know that either." But I had hesitated in my answer and he sensed I wasn't being honest.

"Yes, you do. Please tell me. I have a reason for asking."

"In that case, you must give me your reason first."

"Very well. I'm a doctor. When you were brought into the hospital, I was senior resident and I handled you in the emergency room and kept a tight follow-up on your case. During the time I attended you, you were either unconscious or nearly so."

"So that's it," I exclaimed. "Your face. I've been having a recurring dream and in it your face is above me, as if you were bent over me. I remember now—though vaguely."

"It would be vaguely. You were semi-conscious most of the time and sedated all the time I was there."

"While you were there?"

"I left the hospital ten days after you were admitted. My service was up and I was going into private practice. I came back to look in on you once, but you were asleep. I kept a check on your condition, however."

"Thank you for your concern, Doctor. I know you must have been very kind to me because of that dream that kept recurring."

"I was up with you all night that first day you were admitted."

"Was I that badly hurt?"

"Yes. Your face was cut and in need of plastic surgery, your skull was laid open, a score of bruises and cuts elsewhere."

"Then you saved my life, Dr. Lansing."

"Not just I. It took about thirty of us. From the ambulance men who got you to us in time, to the internists, plastic surgeon, and finally the psychiatrist. Each of us was part of the effort. That's true in every case. No one person can take all the credit."

"Why didn't you introduce yourself when we met in the bookstore?" I asked.

"It was hardly the place for the kind of an explanation I just gave you."

"Is that why you crashed the party? To see how I was progressing?"

"Yes. As I told you, I saw an item in the society column this morning about the party and I thought it was time you met me—now that you've recovered."

I liked this man when he was no more than a face in my dreams. Now that I knew he was real and had not only worked over me and had lost many hours of sleep caring for me—I felt very humble and deeply in his debt.

"Merely to say thank you seems like very little, but at the moment I don't know how else to express my appreciation."

"My reward is seeing you well—except for your loss of memory. Tell me, have you had recall of any kind?"

"Yes," I replied soberly. "I remembered my late husband's playroom—the location of it. Also, the suite occupied by my mother-in-law. You must have met Janet."

"No. At the time I left, you'd still not been identified."

"I see."

"Then you must meet her now. She's most curious."

"She's a handsome woman. I saw you talking with her."

"Yes, she is. Wait until you see Marilyn, her older daughter. They call her their golden girl."

"I believe I have seen her and the description is apt."

"Then there's Nancy, Janet's younger daughter. She'll be at our table."

"I take it Nancy is not a golden girl."

"You might find her more interesting."

"She's the brain," he said. "If you like her, I'll like her."

"I want you to like her. It's what she needs. She has a terrible inferiority complex, and what's worse, I may as well tell you, she said I treated her cruelly before the accident. I want to make amends."

He looked puzzled. "Just how were you cruel?"

"I said things to her that—hurt her. Also, I understand

I neglected my children. And though no one has come out and said it—I learned just an hour ago, I was an alcoholic."

Much to my surprise, he smiled. "You sound like a monster."

"I'm sure I was."

We were both distracted by muted sounds of someone moving on the grass. A moment later we were startled when a guard, holding an enormous dog on a leash, appeared before us.

"I'm sorry, Miss," the guard said. "We've orders to patrol the grounds to make certain no party crasher or thief gets in."

I regarded the animal. "I doubt they'd get very far."

"They wouldn't, Miss," the guard said proudly. "These dogs are well-trained."

Dr. Lansing said, "How can they detect a party crasher or thief from a regular guest?"

"A thief would be easy. He'd be skulking about the grounds. A party crasher, well—getting one of them might be difficult."

"Then I'm safe," Dr. Lansing replied.

The guard chuckled, thinking it rather funny. He moved along then, the animal forcing him almost to a run. Once he was out of sight, we laughed.

"You like your little joke, Doctor," I said.

"I couldn't resist it," he replied. "However, perhaps the joke was on us. He could have been eavesdropping."

"I'm sure you're wrong," I said.

"Nonetheless, I'm bringing you back to the house. Do you really like those dogs around?"

"I hadn't thought about it," I said. "Don't forget— I only returned yesterday."

"Well, think about it—the dogs. I like dogs, but those who have been trained to attack and kill have no place on an estate. Particularly where there are children."

"Of course," I exclaimed. "How terrible of me not to think of that. But I must confess, Doctor, it's difficult for me to think of myself as a mother. I already love the twins. They're very dear and completely unspoiled. But I have absolutely no memory of the past—not even of Larry. I look at his portrait and I'm looking at a stranger.

The only person I recalled when I came here was you and I thought you were a product of my dreams. Either that or you were someone I knew before the accident."

"Anyone in particular?"

"No. I wondered if it might have been someone I went out with, or you were my employer."

"What did you do before the accident?"

"I was a secretary in New York."

"You remember that?"

"No. Janet told me it's where I met my late husband. He flew to New York on business. My employer was a friend of Larry. That's how he met me. We had a whirlwind courtship and I returned here as his bride."

He made no comment, for we'd reached the house. Janet met us inside and I introduced her to Dr. Lansing, explaining how he'd been senior resident when I was brought to the hospital and he had worked on me.

"But how did you happen to be here tonight, Dr. Lansing?" Janet asked after she'd acknowledged the introduction.

"I saw in the morning paper you were giving a small dinner for your daughter-in-law to celebrate her return from the hospital. I must confess I crashed the party."

Janet laughed. "How clever of you."

"Seriously," he added, "I wanted to see how your daughter-in-law was progressing."

"Thank you, Doctor." Janet looked pleased. She turned to me. "Why didn't you tell me about Dr. Lansing?"

"I didn't remember him," I said.

Dr. Lansing said, "I left the hospital to start my private practice ten days after Sandra was admitted. She was sedated during that time and would have no recollection of me."

"True," Janet said. "I'm sorry I didn't know about you so I could have thanked you for all you did."

"Sandra already has," he said.

I wasn't startled at his use of my first name, nor was Janet. I wondered if he had called me Sandra while I was a patient, then remembered I was Jane Doe while he was there.

"Go have your dinner," Janet urged. "I'm still gathering up the guests. Nancy is already there, as are the other two couples who are occupying your table. They'll not intrude. They're much too interested in food."

"Come to think of it," Dr. Lansing said, "it sounds good."

"To me also," I said. "I've not eaten since breakfast."

"Then come along. You can't afford to have a relapse."

I introduced Nancy and the other two couples introduced themselves, then lowered their heads to concentrate on their plates which were laden with food. Most of the tables were occupied and the room buzzed with conversation.

Nancy eyed Dr. Lansing soberly. "Just where did you come from, Doctor dear?"

"Out of nowhere into here," he completed the line.

I was startled at her light banter and apparently showed it, for she laughed. Dr. Lansing seated me and eased himself into the chair alongside me. It was a tight squeeze, but we made it and I was grateful to Janet.

"Don't be shocked, Sandra," Nancy murmured. "I'm a little drunk. I usually get stoned when I get stuck with one of these things. I'd a million times rather be in my lab, playing with my bugs—to quote my dear sister. What do you doctor in, Doctor?" she asked.

"Medicine. General practitioner." His manner was casual, but in the brief time I'd been with him, I knew he was studying her carefully.

"I thought you might be a shrink," she said. "Sandra still needs one."

"No, she doesn't," he replied quietly. "No more than you do."

"Then you think I'm normal," she said.

"When you want to be," he said.

An appetizer of hearts of palm with crab legs was placed before us.

Dr. Lansing said, "Ah," picked up his fork and began to eat.

He'd parried Nancy's verbal jabs skillfully. If she'd expected to irritate him, she'd failed. I was famished and pretended to give my attention to my plate, though watching Nancy guardedly. She said no more, but I was certain I detected respect in her eyes for the doctor.

The rest of the dinner was as delicious and well-prepared as the appetizer. During the remainder of the meal Dr. Lansing and I discussed social changes, ecology and, with great reluctance on his part, his years of study.

I tried to draw Nancy into the conversation twice, but once she realized she couldn't make a scene, she retreated into herself. Before the meal was over, she excused herself and left the table. When Dr. Lansing and I completed our dinner, we excused ourselves, leaving the two couples on their second dessert.

There was more dancing after dinner, but he led me to the staircase. "I can see fatigue etched in your face already and while I'm not your doctor, I'm concerned with your welfare. Go to bed."

"Thank you, Doctor," I replied. "I am tired."

"It was too soon for anything like this, you know."

"Yes," I agreed. "But the family was thinking of me when they did it."

"Before they have another one, have them consult with you first. If you're in doubt, call me."

"Are you serious?"

"Completely. May I call you? I'd like to see you again. Socially, not professionally."

"You may," I said. "And doctor. . . ."

"Yes?"

"I'm glad you crashed the party."

He smiled. "So am I. I enjoyed every moment—even Nancy."

He took one of my hands between both of his, squeezed it gently and bade me a good night. "Run along now. I'll stand here until you reach the top of the stairs. I want to make sure you have no more partying tonight."

"My word," I said, then turned and went up the stairs. I really felt weary and by the time I'd reached the top, I was trembling with weakness. I turned to see if he'd gone and was pleased to observe Janet introducing him to Marilyn, Sidney, and Richie.

I stopped by the twins' room to look in on them. It was in darkness, but the soft light of the bunny light guided my way into their bedroom. Their sleep was peaceful, lending to their look of innocence. I wanted to bend and kiss their brow, yet hesitated. The idea of motherhood still seemed strange to me. I supposed if I ignored the twins before the accident, my uneasiness regarding them was understandable.

I entered my suite and stopped short. Nancy was stretched out on the chaise. There was a glass on the table beside her, filled with alcohol no doubt.

"Hi," she said. Her smile was crooked, her eyes belligerent.

"Hello, Nancy." I repressed a sigh at the sight of her. I was in no mood to engage in verbal fencing. "I'm tired. Would you mind leaving?"

"Can't I even ask how you liked the party?"

"It was a success. Very lovely."

She regarded me curiously. "You mean you remembered someone?"

"No. I really mean it was good of your mother to go to all the trouble with that idea in mind."

"Leave it to Mother. I'm sure she'll consider it a success too. But then, all her parties are. Only this one more than the others."

"Why?" I eased myself into an armchair. I figured I might as well see this through. Nancy made no attempt to leave and I had a feeling she wouldn't until she'd had her say.

She smiled. "If I were to tell you, you'd say I was a dingaling."

"I don't think of you that way."

"Just how do you think of me?"

"As a very lonely person."

Her eyes were scornful. "Don't pity me."

"I'm tired, Nancy, and I'm not going to let you pick a quarrel. You've had too much to drink, but I'll ignore that."

She picked up her glass and took a sip of the liquid. "I guess Sandra Larrabee took the cure while in the hospital."

"I have no recollection of my drinking. Let's get back to the subject of my pitying you. I don't. But if you're not happy living in the house, why don't you leave?"

My question clearly startled her to the point where the drink spilled down the front of her frock. "Do you want me out of here?"

"If you can't behave yourself, yes. I've told you I want

you to like me. Maybe that's asking too much. But even if you can't like me, you can be courteous. If you can't, pack and get out. Now please go. I'm tired to the point of exhaustion."

She set down the glass, wiped her hand on the hem of her gown and stood up, swaying slightly. She'd had more liquor than she could handle. "I'd better not leave tonight. I might get torn apart by the dogs. None of the cars are mine, you know, so I'd have to walk and hitch a ride from some motorist."

"Don't assume a martyr complex," I said. "You're in no condition to drive, but I'll have Gilbert take you wherever you wish to go."

"You're actually putting me out?"

"No," I said wearily. "Nancy, I'm not well, and I'm *so* tired."

"The dogs," she said, as if to divert my attention. "Why do you allow them on the grounds?"

Dr. Lansing had asked the same question. I spoke slowly, choosing my words carefully. "I'll discuss that with the family in the morning. Stay tonight. When you've —rested, we'll talk. I'm sure you could be quite likeable if you wanted to be. You were today when I visited you in your lab."

She moved unsteadily to the mantel, leaning her head against it. "Oh, it's Marilyn who does this to me. She comes on like a four-alarm fire. She walks in a room and —pow! You know what I mean."

"I know. And you've got to accept it. You can excel in the field of science."

"How? The family thinks I'm weird."

"Then get a job in a laboratory. Show them you can be both independent and a worthwhile individual in your own right."

"You do want to get rid of me," she said.

I stood up, went to the door and with my hand resting on the knob, said, "Nancy, I will not argue further with you. Tomorrow think of what we talked about, then let me know what you've decided to do. But if you remain here, you've got to change."

She made no answer, but walked slowly and carefully over to where her glass set. She regarded it intently and her hand half reached out for it, then dropped to her side. I opened the door as she approached. She exited without even glancing at me.

I closed the door, went over to pick up her nearly empty glass and brought it into the bathroom. I rinsed it, wondering if it was a precautionary measure on my part—that I feared if it stood there, I might drink it. Or if the thought of smelling the stale drink in the morning had caused me to empty the glass and rinse it.

I undressed, cleansed my face and went directly to bed. I was exhausted, so much so that not even the face of Douglas Lansing appeared in my dreams. But then why should it? I knew now he was real and there was no longer a mystery concerning him and my mind was no longer troubled as it sought to identify him with my past. He was no part of it. I was glad and I believe I drifted off to sleep with a half smile on my face. He'd said he would call. His interest couldn't be purely professional— at least I hoped it wasn't. It wasn't until the following day I had guilt feelings regarding Larry. How I wished the amnesia which clouded my mind would slip away, allowing my memory to return.

TEN

I awoke with a sense of urgency, as if I'd overslept and must rush to prepare myself for the day. Prepare myself for what? I couldn't imagine, yet I felt the urge was one of habit. I thrust the idea from my mind, showered and dressed, choosing a light woolen slacks suit.

I breakfasted alone, then went to the library to talk with Sid regarding the dogs and also the manner in which the estate was run. Since I'd inherited everything, I felt I should learn what it was all about, though I didn't find the idea particularly exciting.

I tapped on the closed door, heard a chair pushed back and footsteps approach. Sid's sober features brightened in a smile at sight of me.

"Come in, Sandy. You look great this morning."

"I feel great. I'd like to talk with you."

"Good." He stepped back and after I entered, closed the door, explaining, "If the door is open, Janet or Nancy or Marilyn will drift in."

"I don't mind," I told him. "I just want to talk with you regarding a few things which I feel I should know about."

"The estate first," he said. "Do you mind?"

"Not a bit."

"It would take much too long to discuss it verbally. However, there is a detailed list of your assets and holdings in the safe which is behind the hand-tooled leather screen. I'm going to give you the combination to it. Your jewels are in it, and there will be times when you'll wish to wear them."

"They don't interest me at present. I'm concerned with the management of the estate."

"I do that. Larry gave me power of attorney before his death. You were too disturbed then to concern yourself with anything."

"So I've been told. I marvel that you put up with me."

I seated myself in a leather chair. Sid moved around the desk to occupy the tall leather-upholstered swivel chair. He was very handsome in a suave sort of way and he was smartly dressed in a red plaid sports jacket and red slacks.

"You were heading for a breakdown and we were too stupid to realize it. If we had, we'd have kept a closer check on your movements whenever you left the house. Not to spy, but for your own safety. I regret we didn't."

"Don't feel guilty. You couldn't have known my mental condition. But I'm intent on doing my best to bring back my memory. That's why I wanted to talk with you. To learn everything I should."

Sid opened the drawer of his desk and took a slip of paper from it. "Here's a start. The combination to the safe. Open it."

I took the proffered slip of paper and he led me to what seemed like a large black metal wall, though the dial in the center gave mute evidence as to what lay behind it. I carefully turned it to the left and right, to the numbers indicated on the paper. I heard a muted click and tried to pull the door open. Sid smiled and did it for me.

"It's a heavy door and you haven't the strength for it yet," he said.

He snapped a switch and the interior lit up. I was astounded to find myself in an area the size of a room. There were metal cabinets which further protected the contents. Sid used a key to unlock them. He slid various ones open, revealing stacks of important-looking documents. He closed them, locked them, and handed me the key, telling me he had a spare one.

I unlocked another to see more papers. I scanned one briefly, noting it was stock in a diamond mine. Another revealed I was a large holder in an insurance corporation.

"Convinced you're an heiress?" Sid asked.

"Very much so," I stated. "Where are the jewels?"

"On the opposite side."

We crossed the room and Sid pointed out the cabinet. I opened it and even in the dim light I exclaimed in awe at the various pieces which sparkled with a deep radiance. There were diamonds, rubies, pearls, and emeralds made up into earrings, bracelets, necklaces, and pins, nestled neatly on velvet. I closed and locked the cabinet.

"I haven't the slightest recollection of any of it," I said.

"Every piece is yours," Sid said, "though you were always generous about allowing Janet and Marilyn to wear them whenever they wished. Nancy, as you must know by now, has no interest in the glamour bit."

"Oh, that reminds me, who hired the watchdogs?"

I spoke as I opened another cabinet. At first, there seemed to be nothing in it and I almost closed it until a bit of metal attracted my eye. I reached in and my hand closed around a purse. I took it out. It seemed out of place here, being of medium size, of fake leather and certainly, to put it kindly, inexpensive.

"What is this doing here?" I asked.

"That was the purse the boys recovered when they chased the thief who snatched it from you."

"You mean I was carrying this?"

Sid nodded. "When you returned to us after your many disappearances, you never wore any of the clothes you were wearing when you left the house."

"But where did I go?" I exclaimed in alarm.

"We don't know," he replied. "You never talked about it and we made no attempt to pry. Janet wouldn't allow it. She kept hoping you'd snap out of the depression you'd slipped into. I meant to throw that old thing away, but I forgot."

"I'm glad you didn't. It might help me to remember where I went."

Sid spoke hesitantly. "Perhaps it would be better if you—didn't remember."

I opened the purse and saw something metallic in the bottom. I reached for it and discovered they were keys. I regarded them lying on my open palm.

"That's all the purse contained," Sid said. "They don't belong to the doors here."

I said, "Apparently they have something to do with the life I led when I disappeared."

"Why try to remember that part of it?" Sid asked.

I dropped the keys back in the purse, snapped it shut, and slipped the handle over my wrist. "I'm the mother of two adorable girls. If I, at any time, behaved in a way that would prove embarrassing to them and shameful to me, I want to know about it. I'll keep the purse and keys in my possession and look at them frequently. Perhaps, in time, I'll remember."

"What good will it do?" he asked.

"I'll think about that when I discover which locks these keys open."

Sid nodded. "All right, Sandra. Just please, for God's sake, don't get morbid again."

"I'll do my best," I said fervently. "I promise."

He smiled in relief. "I can't ask for more. Now—you asked about the dogs."

"They're vicious, Sid. Frightening, really. And my concern is for the children."

"I know." He seemed to agree with me. "It was Janet's idea. There were prowlers on the estate after Larry died and the extent of this estate became public. Janet's concern is for the twins. She's terrified of kidnapping."

I exclaimed in sudden alarm. "I never thought of that."

"It's worth thinking about," he said. "Especially today."

I couldn't help but agree.

He said, "The men who handle the dogs are competent or they wouldn't be here. However, it's up to you, Sandra. If you wish me to dispense with their services, you need only say the word."

"Oh no, keep them, by all means."

I walked slowly from the safe back to the library, my

mind a jumble of thoughts. I snapped open the purse, dropped the combination into it and went back to my room. I took the keys from the purse, intending to transfer them to the handbag Janet had sent to the hospital for me. I regarded them in the palm of my hand. I was hefting them, as if by doing so I could tell what lock they fitted simply by their weight. One key was quite small, a mailbox type. Why I should know that, I had no idea. The middle-sized key was clearly a car key for it was stamped with the word Chevrolet. The third key was of the type that fits a tumbler lock—a door key, probably. I dropped them into the handbag I was using currently. I would ask Dr. Lansing's advice about them. The keys must have some meaning, but if they didn't belong to any lock on this estate—and I was certain they didn't, or Sid would have known about it—how had I come into possession of them? Had I lived some kind of double life?

Completely frustrated, I tossed the keys into my purse impatiently and snapped the lid shut. Sid had asked me not to become morbid; he was right. I must look ahead, take each day as it came, and hope that with it, a ray of light would penetrate the inner recesses of my mind.

I decided to pay Nancy a visit. After all, sooner or later we were going to have to come to some sort of understanding. I left the house and halfway to her lab I came upon the fenced-in kennel and runway in which four brutal-looking dogs were eying me. They didn't bark, but as I moved along the outside of the runway, they trotted beside me, separated only by that wire fence.

A man with a holstered gun on his hip, wearing a brown uniform, came out of the small cabin at the end of the runway.

"Morning, Mrs. Larrabee," he said politely.

"Good morning. What is your name?"

"Mike Thornley. I work for a protection agency. I'm on days this week. I alternate with Tod Briskin. At night, we both patrol the grounds."

"How many dogs altogether?" I asked.

"Just these four, Mrs. Larrabee," he responded brightly. "They're better than a burglar alarm system."

"Suppose," I said, "I came home very late, on foot. I

opened the gate and the dogs were there. What would happen?"

"They'd attack."

"I couldn't enter my own home then?"

"Not unless one of us was with the dogs to keep them down. We always are unless we hear something and then we turn them loose."

"I see. Thank you, Mr. Thornley."

"You can sleep safely with this kind of protection, Mrs. Larrabee. If anybody should manage to get in, they'd never get out. We patrol all night long."

I thought of the twins. "I admit knowing that does give me greater peace of mind. Thank you again."

I continued on to Nancy's lab. The door was partially open but I could see no one and I knocked lightly on the door frame.

Nancy called, "Come in."

I did and she appeared from what was apparently a bathroom, holding an ice bag on her head. Her eyes were deeply circled.

"Hi," she said and winced. She was really hung over and even the effort to speak was painful. "Have a seat."

"You better have one too."

She chose a straight-back chair, resting her head carefully against its high back. I chose a rocker near the window, looking out on the garden.

"Just don't rock," Nancy said. "I'll get dizzy looking at you."

"I won't." I repressed a smile with difficulty and got to my reason for coming. "Do you remember last night, Nancy?"

"Yes. I was a louse."

"You were rude. Both to Dr. Lansing and to me. You and I had a little talk in my suite afterward. Do you recall that?"

She nodded, then moaned and pressed the ice bag more tightly to her brow. "You issued an ultimatum."

"In a manner of speaking. Have you been able to think about it?"

"I apologize. Does that satisfy you?"

"Not completely."

"I can't get down on my knees. I'll fall over."

93

"I'm sure you would, but I don't expect obeisance, just respect and good manners. Otherwise, you must leave."

"Where would I go?"

"I haven't the faintest idea. Nor do I care." I decided to be as offensive as she, believing I'd reach her better that way. It worked, for her eyes opened slowly and they held a look of surprise.

"You really mean that, don't you?"

"I do."

"Do you want me to go? I mean, do you dislike me the way you did before?"

"I haven't the faintest idea of how I regarded you before, other than what you told me. I gather I wasn't a particularly likeable person."

"You weren't. You've changed."

"Thanks. Can you?"

Our eyes challenged one another. Hers lowered slowly. "I'll change. It won't be easy. I've always made a point of being nasty because I've had to take nastiness. But I like you, I really do. I haven't wanted to. I'm not even sure I want to be likeable, but I'll damn well make the effort."

"I can't ask for more."

The phone rang and once again, Nancy held onto her head. "Please answer it, for God's sake. My head is splitting."

I did. Ethel said, "Oh, Miss Sandra, there's a call for you. I've been trying all over to get you. Decided to try Miss Nancy's lab."

"What is it, Ethel?" I asked.

"Dr. Lansing's on the phone," she said.

"Thank you. I'll take the call."

I heard Ethel hang up, then Dr. Lansing's voice greeted me. He said, "I called to thank you for a pleasant evening. I was wondering if you'd think me terribly vain if I asked you to come and see my office."

"I'd like to."

"I have a light schedule today. How about two?"

"Fine." I was elated we'd be together again so soon. I heard a soft intake of breath. "Was that you, Doctor?"

"No. I wondered if it was you."

"No."

94

The gentle click of a phone being carefully replaced was evident.

His tone was casual, but I sensed his irritation. "Someone was eavesdropping."

"It seemed that way," I replied cautiously. Nancy was eying me speculatively. She no longer held the ice bag to her brow and her interest seemed centered on what I was saying. "Where is your office located, Doctor?"

"On Robertson Boulevard." He gave me the address. I judged it to be not far from the bookstore where we'd met.

"I was going to call you to ask for an appointment. I have a mild headache and have been having them since before I left the hospital. I suppose it's natural, but they are a nuisance."

"I'll prescribe something." He went along with the little game I'd decided to play. "Good-bye for now."

I was annoyed at whoever had been listening in on the call but was careful not to show it. I picked up the phone again and pushed the button labeled garage. Gilbert answered promptly.

"This is Miss Sandra. I shall need a car in time to keep a two o'clock appointment on Robertson Boulevard."

"Yes, madam," he said. "Do you have a preference in cars?"

"None," I said. I was still angry. I walked back to the house slowly, giving myself time to cool off. The most effective way to do that, I discovered, was to anticipate the pleasure of once again being with Dr. Lansing.

I returned to the house and met Ava in the upstairs hall. "Where are the twins, Ava?"

"In school, Miss Sandra," she replied, a look of surprise on her face that I'd not thought of it.

"Of course. How stupid of me. I'll see them later today."

I continued on to my room and checked to see if the keys were still in my purse. They were. I felt a sudden weariness overcome me. I'd been told to expect it, and to give in to it by lying down. I did just that and must have dozed because when I wakened, it was after twelve. I undressed, showered hastily, brushed my hair and coaxed it into curls by running my fingers through it. I had to smile at the result attained with such little effort, for it looked like an expensive styling job.

I selected a pale violet suit, and from the jewelry chest chose darker violet bead earrings with matching bracelet. I saw a hot pink suede purse and matching pumps and transferred my cosmetics, along with the mysterious keys, to that purse. There was no time to lunch and I was too excited to be hungry. I was glad no one was about when I left my room. Gilbert had the Rolls Royce parked before the entrance.

I gave him Dr. Lansing's address and we headed onto Sunset Boulevard after we left the half-hidden entrance to the estate. I tried to be as observant as possible during the trip, studying buildings and names of restaurants and stores to see if any struck a responsive chord in my blacked-out memory. When we reached Dr. Lansing's address, I had not found one place which stirred my memory.

ELEVEN

Dr. Lansing's office was on the second floor of a small building. A somber-faced man occupied one of the chairs in the waiting room. The glass window slid back, revealing an attractive girl in white uniform.

I gave my name and she said, "Oh yes, Mrs. Larrabee. Doctor is expecting you. You'll have a few minutes' wait."

"Thank you." I sat down and picked up a magazine. The nurse opened the door, summoning the somber-faced gentleman. He'd no sooner disappeared then she opened the door and spoke my name.

Dr. Lansing, in a white coat, stethoscope around his neck, looked very professional. The nurse closed the door, giving us complete privacy.

"You look very well, Sandra," he said. "What about those headaches?"

"Completely feigned," I said, smiling.

"Because of the eavesdropper?" he asked.

"Yes," I said. "I can't imagine who'd do such a thing. Of course, it may have been accidental, I don't know. And there's no reason why I shouldn't have stated I had one specific reason for wishing to see you."

He smiled. "I hope it's that you enjoy my company."

I returned the smile. "I do, and I want to talk with you. About me—or my past."

He regarded me with new interest. "You mean you've remembered something?"

"I wish I did."

"That's unusual, you know. Even considering the extent of your injuries, some glimmer of the past should occur."

"What hurts the most is that I don't feel like a mother. I'm already fond of the twins, but I feel no bond. Even with you. Your face haunted me and yet I couldn't recall where I'd seen it."

"But you recognized me in the bookstore."

"Did you follow me in there?"

"Guilty. I saw you walking along the street. I had to get a closer look at you, to speak to you, to hear the sound of your voice. I was hopeful you'd remember me. However, it isn't surprising you didn't."

"I'm so glad though you were real. I was striving desperately to place you from out of my past." I opened my purse and took out the three keys on their key ring. "These were in the purse I was carrying at the time of the accident. My purse was snatched—or did you know?"

"Yes. The police brought it to the hospital. What happened to it after that, I don't know."

"The only thing in it were these three keys. It frightens me to think of what they could represent."

"What do you mean?"

"I understand I behaved strangely after Larry's death. I would leave the house for days at a time. That's why Janet made no attempt to locate me. I always returned, but never wearing the clothes I'd had on when I left."

"Didn't anyone at the house question you about your absences?"

"No. They couldn't very well, since I inherited everything at Larry's death. Also, I'd become very withdrawn. I'd not enter into conversations with the family, not important since Sidney had power of attorney once Larry died. I'm glad he did. No telling what I did during those periods when I was elsewhere."

"And you think these keys are a clue to what you did when you slipped away to be by yourself."

"I can think of no other reason for them and I'm terrified."

He placed a comforting arm about my shoulders. "Don't be. There's probably a very simple explanation for them."

"The purse they were in was very cheap."

"That's no disgrace. Don't upset yourself unnecessarily."

He examined each key singly as I had done, identifying them as to their apparent nature. "A mailbox key, certainly," he said. "And some sort of a door key. The car key is to a Chevy. Do you have one?"

"There is no Chevrolet in my garage. I made certain of that."

"May I keep them for you?"

"If you wish, Doctor."

"You might mislay them and it's possible they have some definite meaning, though not what you fear. How are the twins this morning?"

"I didn't see them. They were taken off to school before I remembered them."

"Are there no flashes of memory at all?"

"Nothing of importance. I did have a feeling I'd been in that bookstore before. That's why I went in, and I thought I knew my way around it rather well, but the proprietor didn't recognize me."

"Did you think he was familiar, even vaguely?"

"Well . . . yes . . . but of course if I'd seen him before, he must have seen me."

"Not necessarily. The man's so in need of eye surgery that he can barely see the books he sells, and if the titles aren't in big print, he can't tell which book is which. He trusts his customers, I guess."

"But what's the difference? I am Sandra Larrabee. That's an established fact."

"Oh yes, definitely," he said. "But still it might be useful if you could remember a friend or an acquaintance."

"I can't. I've tried during my weeks in the hospital."

"Do you ever experience any moments of doubt as to who you are?"

"Never."

"Yet you did remember a couple of things about your home—when you returned to it, I mean."

"Yes," I admitted.

"I want to hear about it again."

"Nothing much. I knew where my husband's room was. That is, his room as a little boy. It had been kept intact over the years. I knew where Janet's suite was. I placed my purse in the drawer I'd reserved for it on my return from the hospital."

"What was your husband's name?"

"Larry. Why?"

"Does it sound familiar when you say it?"

"No, Doctor. Why all these questions?"

"I'm trying to ascertain the degree of your amnesic condition. I'm afraid it's very deep."

"Do you think I'll ever regain my memory?"

He nodded reassurance. "I believe you will."

"When? How long will it take? Even in the short time I've been home from the hospital, there are moments when I feel so frustrated, I want to open my mouth and scream."

"Don't do it. You can hang on. Now—are you free Sunday?"

"Sunday and every day. I must have led a very useless, idle life."

"Don't dwell on that. I'd like to take you to dinner, but first I want to drive you around the various sections of town and see if any section seems familiar."

I shook my head. "I don't know if I want to. I'm frightened about those disappearances."

"Don't be. We must try every means possible to lift the curtain. We'll be looking for places—and faces—that you may recognize. All we need is a beginning."

"That's what Dr. Beardsley told me." I moved to the door. "I'm taking up too much of your time. I'd better go."

He opened a drawer and took out a small envelope. "These are mild headache pills. You can say I prescribed them and told you not to worry."

I placed them in my bag. "Thank you. It was foolish of me to resort to deception to come and see you."

He followed me and took my hand. "Don't let anyone talk you out of our Sunday date. I'll be there at about noon. We'll need considerable time to cruise around."

He escorted me to the door. When he opened it, I saw that his waiting room was comfortably filled and I felt a modest glow of pride that he'd been in practice such a short time and he seemed to be doing well.

Back in the car, I told Gilbert to take me home. During the ride I found myself smiling out of sheer joy because I'd seen Douglas Lansing. I supposed, with a low chuckle, that I was the only girl in the world who'd had a dream man come true. I wondered if I'd had this same warm regard for Larry. The thought nudged my conscience. I was a widow of only a few months' duration. I should not be thinking of another man this way.

When the Rolls pulled up in front of the house, I saw another car parked there. The visitor turned out to be Dr. Beardsley, who welcomed me with a wide smile and an exclamation of delight at my appearance.

"It's good to see you, Doctor," I said.

Janet, standing beside the doctor, said, "I'm relieved you returned while Dr. Beardsley was still here. Now I'll leave you two while the doctor finds out how you're coming along."

"Stay, Janet," I urged. "This is no psychiatric examination. I've no secrets."

"Thanks." She looked pleased.

"How have you been, Sandra? Any weakness, any flashes of memory, any headaches?" Dr. Beardsley asked.

"No weakness and only inconsequential flashes of memory. But I have had mild headaches. In fact, I just came from Dr. Lansing's office." I opened my handbag. "He prescribed these pills and said there's nothing alarming in my condition."

"Dr. Lansing? Who the devil is he?"

"He was the chief resident who treated me in the emergency room," I explained. "Soon afterwards he went into private practice. He was very kind to me. I met him and invited him to a formal dinner we held last evening."

Dr. Beardsley's brow furrowed. "When you don't feel well, come to me. I thought that was understood."

"But why should I bother you with my mild headaches? Wouldn't it be better to see a physician—a general practitioner—for so minor a thing?"

"With you, nothing is minor," he said. "After this, consult me, please." He examined the pills, touched one to his tongue. "Well, I know what these are. Harmless

101

enough, but not very effective. I'll leave you a prescription for something better. And remember to call me. Any time. Your complete recovery is my responsibility."

"Thank you, Doctor," I said. "I'm grateful."

"Are you going to see Dr. Lansing again?"

"Not professionally," I said. "We have a date Sunday. For dinner."

"Sandra," Janet said, "do you think it wise? Larry has been dead such a short time."

"You forget, Mrs. Larrabee," Dr. Beardsley protested, "that Sandra has no memory of your son. She can't be expected to grieve deeply for a man she cannot recall. And I think seeing another young man is good therapy for her. I want her to get about."

"You're right, of course," Janet said.

"Well, you look and act fine," Dr. Beardsley said. "No need for an examination. The headaches will go away. Don't worry about them."

"I won't," I said cheerfully. "Thank you for dropping by."

"I owed you the visit," he told me. "I came to express my gratitude for that Grecian head you sent me. It's fabulous. I'll treasure it, Sandra."

Janet and I saw him to the door. After I closed it, I took Janet's elbow and brought her back to the drawing room.

"I'm sorry about the way I act," I said. "About Larry, I mean. He was your son and I realize how you must respect his memory. Please try to understand I don't remember him. I can't remember having the twins, but they are adorable and I'm proud to be their mother. But you have to excuse the way I behave. I can't help it."

"I know, Sandra, and I ask that you be tolerant of me." She caught my hand and squeezed it lightly. "Tell me about Dr. Lansing."

"I don't know him very well yet, but I'm indebted to him for his kindness. I regard him as a friend."

"Good." She seemed satisfied. "I only ask that you use discretion in view of your widowhood."

"I'll be discreet," I promised. "Do you know if Sidney is busy?"

"He's not here. He had to go into town on business."

"I meant to talk to him again and get a better idea of what this estate entails, but it can wait. Does Sidney take care of all the details? Paying the servants and other bills? Handling whatever transactions are necessary?"

"Yes, everything. Did you wish to make any changes?"

"Not immediately. But I do think I should have some part in it."

"That you must take up with Sidney. He's managed things for a long time and is expert at it. There is one matter I wish to call to your mind, Sandra dear. The vault in the library is to be kept locked at all times."

"Of course."

"Don't you recall leaving it unlocked?"

"Good heavens, no. I haven't been in the vault since this morning when Sid gave me the combination."

"He told me about it and he also told me he spun the dial after you left. But after lunch when he went in, the door was opened wide. He checked the jewelry, but nothing was missing. Then he noticed the drawer in which he'd placed your black purse was slightly ajar. The purse I brought from the hospital was in it."

"But I didn't go back there," I protested. "I wouldn't even remember the combination."

Her smile was one of reproof. "The combination was in the bag. You must have put it in there when you placed the purse in the metal cabinet."

"But I don't remember. . . ." I said, aghast at the idea of such a mistake.

"No one saw you, but Sidney said you did take the purse with you and it was back in the vault when he checked. Try to remember to keep it locked."

"I will," I said, puzzled and distraught at the thought I could do such a thing. Was I not only completely ignorant of my past, but now beginning to have no awareness of my behavior?

Once alone in my suite, I thought back to my talk with Sid. After leaving him, I came directly upstairs. I took the keys from the bag and must have absent-mindedly dropped the combination into it. I placed the bag in the drawer, took the one I'd used and dropped the keys into it. When I changed my costume, I'd selected

103

another purse and transferred the contents from one bag to another. I must have placed the blue bag back in the drawer. If so, the black one must have been there and surely I'd have noticed it.

I walked into the bedroom and stopped abruptly. The blue bag set on the white bedspread where I'd left it. I hadn't replaced it in the drawer. Yet when could I have done such a thing? Then I remembered having felt fatigue and lying down. I'd drifted off into sleep. Could I have risen then, got the purse from the drawer, brought it downstairs, opened the vault, turned the key in the cabinet, placed the purse in it—or had I locked the cabinet when I took the purse out—I couldn't remember. But I must have done it, then walked out, leaving the safe door open.

I pressed my fingers hard against my mouth. I wanted to cry out, to shout I couldn't have done such a thing, yet I had. I went to the drawer in which I'd placed the black purse. I pulled it open. The drawer was empty. The black purse was down in the safe, but not with the keys. Nor did I have them. I was glad Dr. Lansing had them. At least, I'd not disposed of them in some foolish fashion. I was glad Janet had made no reference to them. I suppose she attached no importance to them.

But the purse was gone! I sat down slowly, wishing it was Sunday so I could discuss this with Dr. Lansing. It might be of no importance, just a temporary slip of memory, but it worried me. If I lost the present as well as the past to the limbo of amnesia, I was in a bad way.

TWELVE

Saturday seemed interminable. I sought out Sid, but was told he had flown to San Francisco about some real estate holdings I had there. Janet had taken the twins to their dancing class; Richie had gone to his country club for a golf foursome. When I went to Nancy's laboratory, my knock was unanswered. I didn't know if she was inside or she too had gone somewhere. Ava informed me Marilyn was at the hairdresser's. She went three times a week, which accounted for her being so beautifully turned out.

I was very restless and strolled aimlessly about the estate. I couldn't even take a ride anywhere because Gilbert was chauffeuring Janet and the twins. I returned to the house and went on an inspection tour of the rooms, with the exception of the upstairs suites which were occupied by the family.

One of the wings was apparently used only for guests, for the rooms, though spotless, were devoid of any personal belongings. The closets were empty. Curious, I opened a few of the drawers. They too were empty, except for the bottom one which contained a photograph album.

I took it out and was pleased to see it contained pictures of the twins from the time of birth. I became excited as I continued to turn the pages, hoping to find a group photo of Larry and me with the twins. However, I wasn't so lucky. For the first time, it occurred to me that except for the painting of Larry over the mantel in our suite, I'd seen no photographs of the family.

On impulse, I went to Janet's suite and even without a glance behind me to see if I was observed, I opened the door and entered the room.

A careful look assured me it was empty. The room was decorated with plastic furniture. A pink rug covered the floor. Very modern and quite interesting. I looked around for a photograph of any kind, but the room was devoid of one. Her bedroom was equally lacking a picture of either her or Richie. I moved on to the suite Marilyn shared with Sidney. It too was done in modern, though with more of a Chinese motif, a few pieces and lots of space. Beautiful and impressive—but with no trace of a family picture.

I dared not go to Nancy's room. I knew full well she'd resent it should she discover me there. But knowing her, I doubted she would collect family photographs. I moved on to the twins' room. Photos of them in their dancing costumes graced one wall. Other than that, I found nothing. A search of their drawers was equally fruitless. I made a mental note to ask Janet if there weren't some pictures of Larry and me. Certainly, a wedding photograph.

I waited in the drawing room, scanning magazines and pacing restlessly, but it wasn't until the dinner hour when Janet returned with the twins. They were tired, but filled with talk of what had transpired at the dancing school, followed by luncheon at a department store in Beverly Hills and after that a trip to the zoo. Their fatigue was obvious, for they yawned several times while telling me. But they were warm and affectionate and it was with a sense of reluctance I let Ava take them upstairs for their dinner.

Janet sighed and kicked off her shoes. She stretched out on a divan before the fireplace. I sat facing her.

"I love them," she said. "But they exhaust me."

"I could have taken them."

She apparently sensed reproof in my voice for she said, "I hope you're not annoyed with me, Sandra."

"No," I said. "But after all, they are mine and I'm trying desperately to feel some bond between them and me. How can I when on their only day home, I don't even get a chance to see them?"

"You shall have them all day tomorrow," she promised. "By yourself."

"I won't have tomorrow with them," I said.

"But the entire family will be here and if you can spare us the time, we can reminisce about the past—the past you can't remember. The children were invited out, but I'll cancel it."

"Please don't. I'm going out tomorrow with Dr. Lansing," I said.

"You could cancel." I sensed reproof in her voice. "I wish you would."

"Ordinarily, I would," I said. "But it's a dinner engagement."

"That won't be until evening."

"He invited me for an afternoon ride along the coast. It's part of the therapy of my remembering."

"Dr. Beardsley is your therapist," she reminded me.

"I know. But I doubt he'd take Sunday afternoon off to drive me up the coast."

"Any one of us could, but on a Sunday afternoon the Pacific Coast Highway is worse than the Abominable Snowman."

"I suppose it is," I said, smiling. "But Dr. Lansing was so kind to me in the hospital, I don't want to call and cancel the appointment."

She eyed me thoughtfully. "Are you serious about him?"

"I hadn't thought about that. And I won't while I'm suffering from amnesia."

"There's also Larry to think of. You've been widowed less than nine months."

"I can't remember him," I exclaimed impatiently. "I can't remember anything."

She sat up, her face contrite. "I'm sorry, Sandra. I'm *also* forgetting, but the fact is that you are an heiress and Dr. Lansing is just starting out in practice."

"Surely you're not suggesting he's a fortune hunter."

"I suppose that's exactly what I am suggesting."

"He's a gentleman and I'm sure his social ethics are as high as his professional ethics."

"Forgive me. I should have confidence in your judgment," she said. "And I will."

"I wish I had as much confidence in my character."

"What are you talking about?"

"My disappearances before the accident. Where did I go? What did I do? How did I live—or conduct myself? And why was it that on my return, I was never wearing the clothes I'd had on when I left?"

Janet sighed. "Who told you about the clothes?"

"Sidney. And I'm glad he did. I want to know everything about myself, no matter how bad it is."

She was shocked at the insinuation. "I'm sure he didn't say there was anything bad about it."

"No," I replied. "But I know I drank. I believe I did say unkind things to Nancy about herself. You lied when you said not to heed anything she said, didn't you? And you lied when you said I was a devoted mother."

"Please, Sandra, you're becoming very agitated."

"Didn't you?" I demanded.

"All right. I lied." She lowered her eyes and voice which had raised as mine had. "Sometimes you overimbibed. It was then—and only then—you suffered a change of personality."

I covered my face with my hands. "I must have been rotten."

"You weren't. You didn't tease Nancy any more than Marilyn did—and still does."

"In that case, I don't blame Nancy for being obnoxious."

"Who's obnoxious?"

I uncovered my face. Marilyn, looking beautiful, poised, and radiant, had entered the room.

Janet said, "Nancy."

"She certainly is," Marilyn said. "But we've learned to live with it."

I slapped the arms of the chair with my hands. "I didn't say Nancy was obnoxious."

"She is, though." Marilyn, quite complacent, sat down beside her mother. "And she does it deliberately. Needles me, dresses in outrageously bad taste, is rude to our guests and hates each of us."

I said, "I don't hate Nancy. And I don't think she hates me."

Marilyn said, "She did before the accident."

"Please girls," Janet implored, "don't quarrel."

"I'm not quarreling, Mother." Marilyn's voice was apologetic. "I'm only telling the truth."

"I don't want Sandra upset," Janet said. "We must bear in mind she doesn't remember anything. I wish she hadn't been told anything about herself before the accident."

"I'm the one to apologize," I said. "I want to know everything about me, yet I'm filled with guilt and shame and fear—particularly in regard to those periods when I would disappear for days at a time."

"Of course you are," Marilyn said kindly. "And I didn't mean to upset you. We were thoroughly lectured by Dr. Beardsley about not doing that."

I sighed. "If only even one answer would come. But nothing. My mind is blank and I find myself fearing to be alone because I can't remember anything."

Marilyn nodded. "It's difficult and nerve-racking. Tell you what. Tomorrow we'll make it a point to be with you the entire day. We'll have a barbeque on the terrace behind the house. We used to do it frequently when Larry was alive. He loved it."

Janet smiled in remembrance.

"Did I?" I asked.

"Of course," Janet said, but her voice was high-pitched and I felt she spoke before Marilyn could.

"Tell me the truth, Janet," I said.

"Darling," her voice was almost pleading. "I don't want you to worry."

"I promise I won't. But please—the truth."

Marilyn said, "You've got to tell her, Mother."

Janet bit at her lower lip. She was pushing the cuticle of each fingernail back with her thumbnail. She was nervous and uncomfortable and I had the feeling she wanted to run from the room.

She spoke finally. "Very well. You did not like anything pertaining to domesticity."

"Did I love Larry?"

Again she hesitated. "We thought you did—at first. And I kept hoping you did, because he worshipped you."

My sigh was one of self-disgust. "How can you bear me in this house?"

Marilyn said, "We're grateful *you* allow *us* to stay."

"Did I ever order you out?" I asked in dismay.

Janet nodded. "Not until after Larry's death and you weren't yourself."

Marilyn said, "Why must you keep asking questions that do nothing but upset you? You're not helping yourself, Sandra."

"I know," I said. "Yet I can't stop asking. There's something else that puzzles me. There are no family pictures around. Just the portrait of Larry. Why is that?"

Janet and Marilyn exchanged looks. Marilyn said, "You might as well tell her, Mother."

"What did I do to them?" I asked.

"You did nothing," Janet said. "One night you and Nancy had a bitter quarrel. You ordered her off the premises."

"Was I drunk?"

"No." Once again Janet's denial came too hastily.

"Tell the truth, Mother. Sandra's entitled to it. What happened wasn't her fault."

"All right," Janet said. "You'd had too much to drink and quarreled with Nancy. In spite, she gathered up every family picture around and destroyed them. She said it was bad enough having to live with us, without having to look at family pictures stuck in every corner of the room."

"The twins' pictures are on the wall of their playroom," I said.

Janet nodded. "And I managed to hide an album in one of the rooms in the guest wing."

"But all that's in the past," Marilyn protested.

My smile was bitter. "If you're asking me to forget it, I have. If only I could remember one little thing."

Marilyn said, "The only thought I have now is one of hunger."

Janet glanced at her watch. "It's time for dinner."

I said, "I'd like to be excused, please. I have a headache."

110

Janet said, "May I send you up a tray?"

"No, thanks," I said. "If I want anything later, I'll come down."

"You don't know how to prepare anything," Marilyn said patiently. "You can't even boil water."

"Then it's about time I learned," I said.

I excused myself and went up to my suite, feeling quite dispirited. I slipped out of my dress and lay down. I don't know how long I'd been there, but I apparently had dropped off to sleep, for when I wakened, I was curled up into a ball to ward off the cold. I stirred myself, got to my feet and went to the window. My window faced the east and the morning sun was just appearing over the horizon. I must have been so emotionally exhausted that I'd slept the night through. I went into the bathroom and drew a hot tub. My muscles felt still and I was cold. The bath would waken and relax me.

While I bathed, I recalled how the argument had started. It concerned Janet having taken the twins off for the day. In the discussion which ensued, I'd completely forgotten about them. I again chided myself for my laxity. Yet how could I be expected to act like a loving and devoted mother when I'd ignored them before? Could that be the reason my mind sought vainly to identify with them, to seek a tie of some sort, however small, to link them to me and to my heart?

Then I remembered something. Janet had told me how I'd dressed to please Larry during his illness. It didn't make sense in view of what I'd just learned. I chose an ankle-length skirt with matching vest over a blouse as my costume for the day. Then I went downstairs, pleased to see Janet, lovely in a gossamer peignoir, already there and breakfasting.

She rang for Dicie who nodded when she saw me and retreated to the kitchen, returning with a platter of bacon, eggs, and fried potatoes, plus a tall glass of freshly squeezed orange juice. It was so refreshing I could have smacked my lips over it.

Janet looked wan, as if she'd spent a sleepless night. "I wish I hadn't had to tell you all that yesterday."

"I'm glad you did," I said. "I'll make every effort

not ever to return to my old ways. But there is one thing that puzzles me."

"Oh, Sandra, please," she exclaimed. "I can't take any more."

"Just one question."

"Very well." She set down her coffee cup as if to give me her complete attention.

"Why was I told, when I first came home, I was devoted to Larry during his illness?"

Her smile was one of relief. "You were."

"But it doesn't fit in with what you told me yesterday."

"I know. Once you learned he had a brain tumor, you became the girl he brought back from New York with him. You were devoted to him, scarcely leaving his side. After he died, you resumed drinking—you'd stopped completely during his illness—and it was then you started being absent from here for varying periods. Sandra, please don't upset yourself. When Richie and I talked with Dr. Beardsley and told him about your behavior before the accident, he informed us you were heading for a complete mental breakdown and were probably in the early phases of it. He said your behavior was due to a guilt complex regarding Larry. You blamed yourself for his illness, that he'd worried and brooded about you. But you were completely blameless. Remember that and concentrate on it."

"But I'm filled with self-reproach."

"Try not to be. That won't help you. You're very changed. So far as we're concerned, everything is perfect except your loss of memory." She picked up the platter and held it for me. I helped myself to a generous serving of bacon and two eggs, plus fried potatoes. Having skipped dinner, I was famished.

She said, "So long as you won't be here today, I'd like your permission to take the twins to Sunday School. Also, they've been invited to a birthday party which will also be a barbeque with adults attending. I was going to ask you to join us."

"I'd like to, but I feel it would be unfair to disappoint Dr. Lansing."

"Marilyn asked to come," Janet said. "We'll miss you."

"I'll visit with the twins after breakfast."

"Splendid." Janet touched the napkin to her lips. "Will

you excuse me? I'll just have time to bathe and dress."

I finished my breakfast and drank three cups of coffee. Then I went upstairs. The twins, still in nighties, squealed with delight when I entered their room. Ava and I helped them to bathe and dress and I went downstairs with them. Marilyn and Janet came down shortly. Gilbert already had the car in front. The group of us went outside and I waved a farewell, with the twins waving madly in return.

Once they passed through the gate, I went back inside, returning to my suite. I had no wish to converse with Richie or even Nancy. I was too filled with concern regarding the type of person I'd been and if, once my memory returned, I would revert to my former ways. I waited impatiently for Dr. Lansing to call for me, wanting desperately to talk with him. To tell him about myself and to ask his advice.

THIRTEEN

The tension I'd been filled with slipped away from me once I was in Dr. Lansing's car and we were skimming along Sunset Boulevard.

"Was anything said since I last saw you, or did you come upon anything in that house that has helped to jolt your memory a little?"

"Not a thing. I made a tour of the house yesterday, looking for family photographs. I hoped to find one of Larry and me. I've seen a painting of him, but I thought a picture of us together might reach me somehow. I couldn't find one."

"That's strange."

"I thought so, but when I looked for pictures of the rest of the family, there were none either. I did find an album of the twins in one of the rooms in the guest wing and there are pictures of them in their dancing costumes on the wall of their nursery."

"Did you inquire about it?"

"Yes. And I learned more about myself—none of it good."

I related what I'd been told and though I thought it

would be difficult to repeat, it wasn't. It seemed as if I was talking about another person.

When I finished, he said, "Don't dwell on it." He made a turn off Sunset. "This is Beverly Glen Boulevard. At the top of the mountain are a number of new houses, a fire station, plus an exciting panoramic view of the city when there's no smog."

The road was narrow and curvy and I thought I'd not care about driving it too frequently. As we reached the top, we came upon some newly built homes. They were large, but with land at a premium—somehow I knew that—they were built so close to one another, it was impossible to tell if the houses were attractive because the effect was one of clutter. At the top, he slowed and I looked around.

I said, "I don't recall this."

"Don't be discouraged," he said cheerfully. "We're going back and we'll try Santa Monica. We'll head down to Wilshire. Perhaps something there will strike a familiar chord. Since you've been out here some time, you must have driven over the route frequently. Don't talk now. Just look."

He drove along Wilshire Boulevard, turning off into Westwood Village. We toured the streets slowly and while I didn't feel a stranger to it, I couldn't pick out a store or building that bore a familiar look. He drove back to Wilshire then and I searched vainly for something that would shock me into remembering. We passed from Los Angeles into Santa Monica, a green sign with the name of the city modestly displayed on a post.

"City by the Sea," I exclaimed.

He looked pleased. "How did you know that?"

"I don't know. It just came."

"Were you brought here since you returned from the hospital?"

"I don't believe so."

"Can't you be sure?"

"No."

"Why not?"

I told him then about my replacing the old purse in the safe and leaving the door open, yet having no recollection of having done so.

115

"Did you have the combination to the safe?"

"Yes. Sid had given it to me only that morning. Janet found the combination in the purse."

"What else have you learned about yourself?"

I related everything I'd been told. From time to time, he interrupted me, asking pertinent questions.

"Does the fact that I put the purse back in the safe without remembering having done so, mean I'm losing the ability to remember doing things since the accident?"

"I wouldn't say so. At least, not at this point. I'm going to drive up and down some of these residential streets. We might pass a building that will ring a bell."

He drove up one street to Montana Avenue, then made a turn that would bring us back to Wilshire. After a few blocks, he turned up another side street as far as Montana, and after proceeding a few blocks, again turned down a street that led to Wilshire Boulevard. Both sides of this street were shaded with Indian laurel trees and it was lined with apartment houses. He lessened his speed to allow me to observe them.

We crossed one intersection, reached another. On the corner was a two-story apartment house, one corner of the building done in redwood, the rest stucco. It had a glassed-in entrance way, and as we moved slowly by, I could see a patio garden inside.

I said, "Stop!"

His foot hit the brake hard enough to jolt me forward. "Is it familiar?" he asked anxiously.

"I don't know." I was trying to think, to force away the fog that filled my brain. "The redwood corner. I think I've seen that before . . . and the low steps. Yes! A car came out of the side street once, just missed being hit by another, and wound up on the steps. I thought it was going to end up in the patio."

He eased the car to the curb and shut off the motor. "Where were you when the accident occurred?"

"I don't remember. But I witnessed the accident."

"You said you thought the car was going into the patio. Can you describe it?"

I closed my eyes in an attempt to visualize it. "No."

"But you know there's a patio there."

Doubt began to assail me. "I'm not sure. I think there

116

is, but I couldn't say for certain. Yet the building is familiar and I remember the accident."

"Who was injured?"

"An elderly gentleman. The ambulance came and took him to the hospital. That's all I remember."

"Let's have a look inside," he suggested.

We crossed the sidewalk and went up the few steps. He pushed open the glass door and entered a short corridor leading into the patio. To our left was a row of mailboxes —fifteen of them—designating the number of tenants in the building.

He reached into his pocket, took out the three keys I'd found in the purse and handed them to me.

"See if the small one opens the mailbox," he suggested.

I took the key and without hesitation I thrust it into number 15. The mailbox door opened, but the interior was empty. I closed it, locked it again and turned about to face Doug. I was trembling.

"I found the right box immediately. I . . . must have known which box the key fit."

He held out his hand for the keys. "Now let's see if anybody recognizes you. The manager's apartment is number 5. Here's what I want you to do. Stand directly in front of the door and ring the bell. When it opens, don't say anything. If you recognize the manager, try not to give it away. Let's see if he knows you."

I clung to his arm. "Doug, I'm getting scared. If I ever lived here, what am I doing in that mansion with all that money?"

"You may have lived here before your marriage. If so, maybe we can find some old friends who may help restore your memory."

"Wait, Doug! I never lived in Santa Monica. Janet told me Larry met me in New York where I worked in an office as a secretary."

"Perhaps you knew someone who did live here. Or maybe this was the place you came to during your absences from the house. There could be several reasons why you'd have these keys. They may have no meaning. These mailbox keys are common. The locks are not intricate. It's conceivable one key would fit many of these little doors."

117

I said, "I'm beginning to feel uneasy without knowing why. Do you know anything I don't?"

We had reached the manager's door. Doug said, "Ring the bell." There was no time to wonder if he'd deliberately evaded my question. My finger depressed the button. After a few moments the door opened and a bald-headed, bleary-eyed man regarded me. He wore trousers, but was naked from the waist up.

"Well?" he asked.

I tried to speak, but my mouth was too dry. Doug took over for me.

"We're looking for a Mrs. Blanchard. We were told she's been living here for five or six years."

"Nobody here by that name, mister." He began to close the door. Doug thrust out his foot to keep it open.

"Have you been here that long?"

"I been here goin' on ten. When I say there ain't nobody by the name of Blanchard, there ain't. You see it on the mailboxes?"

Dr. Lansing said, "No. I'm sorry we disturbed you."

The manager mumbled something and closed the door. Dr. Lansing looked at me with the obvious question in his eyes.

I shook my head. "I never saw him before, as far as I can tell."

"Well, it was worth a try," he said. He was still holding the keys and he regarded the door key. "I wonder. . . ."

"Let's try it," I said.

Dr. Lansing kept his voice low. "It shouldn't be difficult since the manager's apartment has no windows or sliding door looking onto the patio."

Our footsteps were muted, for the steps had some sort of rubber composition on them, as did the walkway.

"Should the key turn the lock, we won't go in," he said. "We don't want to get picked up on a burglary charge."

Number 15 was on the second floor, off a balcony that went around the entire building. It was typical of an apartment house of this kind. There was a fountain, a few statues, a well-kept, colorful flower garden and a tree that was beginning to threaten the entire patio area with the spread of its branches. We went up the stairs and along the balcony to the door with the proper number on it.

Dr. Lansing rang the bell and we held our breaths. For once we were in luck. Nobody answered. He inserted the key slowly and quietly. He turned it so it made no sound. The door opened easily. He withdrew the key, closed the door again and we left. If a tenant saw us do that, he would be within his rights to call the police and I certainly wanted no publicity about this. Especially not with Dr. Lansing involved.

We returned to the car. Doug said, "Now the only key left to check is the one to a car, probably a Chevy. I think we should let that wait. We've pushed our luck far enough for now."

I pressed my fingertips to my temples. "It's there, but it won't come through. Yet I have a feeling I'm familiar with that apartment house. There's a laundry room in the garage . . . it has two washing machines and two dryers. . . ."

Dr. Lansing reached over and grasped both my wrists, drawing them down from my face. "Don't try too hard. It will come back. We've made a start. And we did it with the keys."

"No," I contradicted. "I recognized this apartment house. Thanks for driving me around."

"I'm twice as pleased as you," he said. "I had a feeling that once you were in familiar surroundings, you'd start to get recall." He sensed my doubt for he said, "What is it?"

"When I returned from the hospital, I remembered Larry's playroom—Janet kept it intact. I also knew which door opened into her suite. But I never remembered anything else about the house. So, recognizing this building doesn't mean too much."

His lips pursed thoughtfully. "I'm still not discouraged."

"I must have lived in that apartment house after Larry's death. But why didn't the manager recognize me? It's terrible not to be able to remember. And then again, perhaps it's as well. I may have done something or lived in some way that would fill me with self-loathing were I to know."

"I'd lay odds you're worrying about something completely alien to your character," he said. "But until you know exactly what your connection with this apartment house is, stop brooding on it. We're going to head for Malibu now. I know of a restaurant that's not on the water, but you get a view of the Pacific that's breathtaking. Also, it's quiet and restful."

He started the engine and moved slowly away from the curb. I remembered the need for caution. Cars used it as a through street because of the traffic light on the next corner. I also thought about the location of the garage entrance. It was on the side street. As he started down the street, I looked over. A cry of surprise escaped me as I caught sight of Nancy, wearing jeans and a suede fringed jacket. At sight of the car, she darted into the garage.

"What is it?" Dr. Lansing asked.

"Nancy," I exclaimed. "I'll swear I saw her. I wonder if she followed us."

"You recognized her car?" he asked.

"No. She was standing at the garage entrance. I wanted to check to see if I was right about it being on the side of the building. I was. She ducked into the garage when she spotted me—or your car."

"I hope she doesn't suspect you saw her," Dr. Lansing said. "We won't backtrack to pounce on her. I think it's far more interesting to discover she's keeping an eye on you."

"Why?"

"I don't know exactly, but there must certainly be a reason for it. If she thinks you're not on to her, it will be easier to keep her under surveillance."

"You're right."

We were moving along Wilshire now and without any warning, Dr. Lansing made a left turn before oncoming traffic. I cried out in alarm.

"Relax," he said. "We were safe enough, but speaking of being kept an eye on, I think we have a tail."

I started to turn around, but Dr. Lansing warned me against it. "I don't want him to suspect I know he's following us. I'm not sure he is, but he nearly got clipped making the left turn and he's behind us now. I'm going to take Santa Monica Boulevard for a bit, then head back to Wilshire. Look around and pretend you're enjoying the ride."

"I am," I said. "I just wish questions would stop popping into my mind."

"Let them pop. Any day now the answers may also pop into your mind."

"I hope so."

He made a right turn and continued on to Wilshire, proceeding until he reached Ocean Avenue. There he made a right turn, continued to the end and again, to my surprise, turned into the underground garage of a large apartment house.

"I'm pretty sure we gave him the slip. He got stuck by a light and slow Sunday traffic." Doug pulled into an empty stall and turned the ignition key. "We'll park here for a while. He'll probably go on to Malibu, but he'll be ahead of us."

"Why would we be shadowed?"

"I'm wondering if the Larrabees hired a private detective agency to sort of watch over you."

"Without telling me?"

"You're an heiress and, as such, ripe for kidnapping."

"Also," I said, knowing he was too kind to do so, "they remember my disappearances before the accident."

"I wasn't thinking of that."

Without a moment's hesitation, I leaned over and kissed him on the cheek. "Thank you, Dr. Lansing."

"Make it Doug, please. And thank *you*." He was smiling the smile I'd dreamed of so frequently before I knew he was a flesh-and-blood human being.

"The pleasure was mine," I said.

"No," he contradicted, "mine. I've been wanting to do that since the moment you got in the car, but I didn't want my face slapped."

We both laughed then and he said, "Sit closer to me."

I thought of Janet. "I mustn't. I've been a widow less than nine months."

Firmness crept into his voice. "But you *are* a widow. And I'm sure your late husband wouldn't object to your having a little happiness."

I said, "I'm told he was very wonderful and very devoted and I was the direct opposite until I learned of his terrible

121

illness. Then I made every effort to make up for my—weaknesses."

"Don't refer to that again until you've regained your memory. Accept nothing as fact until then. I don't want your mind burdened with guilt feelings. It will interfere with what we're trying to do."

He started the motor, backed out of the stall and headed for the street. "I imagine we've shaken off our shadow. It was a gray sedan with a bad dent in the front right fender. Watch for it. He might pick us up somewhere."

And so we made the ride to Malibu, both of us seeking out the gray car, neither of us catching a glimpse of it. The restaurant, quite picturesque, resembled a chalet and it set high on one of the canyon roads, commanding a magnificent view of the Pacific which was dotted with sailboats. Doug told me they were having a regatta of some kind. However, the breeze had died down and the boats were stranded, waiting for it to come up again.

We were given a window table, well shaded from the late afternoon sun by overhanging eaves. Doug ordered cocktails and we sipped them leisurely, watching the boats still idling. From time to time, one would start a motor and head back to the marina in Los Angeles, their starting point.

"Did the family know I was taking you out?"

I nodded. "I told them."

"Hope they didn't mind."

"Why should they?" I asked, though I lowered my eyes when I spoke.

"You know," he said smiling, "you're just no good at deceit. Who objected?"

"Janet," I said, returning the smile. "She reminded me I was a widow. I had to remind her I couldn't remember ever having been married. However, she has a point."

"She might if the situation were different, but my intentions are honorable. Sandra, I'm in love with you and I want to marry you."

I regarded him with amazement.

"I know I'm blunt," he said. "But a doctor has precious little time to press his case. I love you, Sandra. I loved you before you were ever aware of me. I left the hospital

122

loving you. It was only when I returned to inquire about you and learned you were an heiress, that I felt it was hopeless."

"You couldn't have felt it was completely hopeless or you wouldn't have sought me out."

He smiled. "I'm afraid my resolve wasn't as strong as I'd hoped. When I saw you walking along Robertson, all I could think of was that I had to hear you speak. I'd never heard the sound of your voice. Once I did, I couldn't stay away from you. Yet you know I have nothing. I know you're reputed to be an heiress."

"So they say. I'd give it all up if I could just say I returned that love and would be honored to be your wife."

"But you don't love me."

"I'm afraid I do." He reached across the table for my hand, but I slipped it free of his grasp. "Only so long as I have amnesia and don't know the real me, I'd be taking an unfair advantage."

"Then I'll have to work harder to bring about your total recall—and I will. I want you to be my wife."

"I hope the day will come when I can say yes. If it ever does—and if you have the patience to wait—ask me again."

"I will. Now we'll have dinner."

The menus were brought, and since the restaurant specialized in sea food, we ordered lobster, with a salad as a starter. During the meal, I insisted Doug tell me about himself. He was a native Californian, whose father had been a doctor, though not in Los Angeles. However, his parents were both deceased and except for a maiden aunt who lived in New York City, he had no relatives. I told him that somehow, I felt I had none either. Up until now, I hadn't even thought to ask Janet about it. I made a mental note to do so and hoped I'd not forget. I seemed to have a habit of letting little things slip from my mind. Or doing something I had no awareness or remembrance of—such as replacing the purse in the safe and leaving the door open.

It was dark when we left the restaurant, but there was a glorious full moon whose beams were reflected in the ocean, making it seem like a golden carpet which spread across the water almost to my feet.

Halfway home, Doug's arm enclosed my shoulders and he drew me close. I didn't protest and I did rest my head on his shoulder.

The gate was locked, but he got out and rang. In no more than a minute, one of the men with two dogs on a leash, appeared. He opened the gate from the inside after making certain of my identity and Doug drove me up to the door. There he tilted my head and kissed me. I didn't attempt to move away from him, for my heart seemed to leap at the contact and I wondered how I could resist, were he to repeat his proposal. Yet I knew I must and, knowing that, I slid across the seat and opened the door.

"I'll keep in touch with you," he said. "And remember to be cautious. Today we were followed."

"Did you get a look at the driver?" I asked.

"He was about fifty, a heavy-set individual with dense black eyebrows set in a square-shaped face."

"I'll remember."

"Take care," he urged. "If anything concerns you or if you see that individual, please call me immediately."

"I will. I'll keep an eye on Nancy also."

"Might be a good idea."

FOURTEEN

Janet, Richie, Marilyn, and Nancy were assembled in the drawing room. They were sipping sherry and Richie poured me a glass. I really didn't want it, but they seemed pleased to see me—all except Nancy, who seemed less hostile than indifferent.

Janet said, "The twins waited up for you, but they finally got so sleepy, we had to send them off to bed."

"I'm sorry I missed them. I'll make it up to them tomorrow."

"Good." She settled back in her chair.

Marilyn was curled up in her usual corner of the divan. She wore a soft green satin hostess gown that shimmered with her slightest movement. She set her empty glass down on the cocktail table and settled back. Nancy, on the floor, was using a marble fireplace to support her back. She was sipping wine also and had the carafe beside her. Richie, seated on the stool, reached down for the carafe to refill his glass. She held out her hand until he gave it back to her. Her glass was full. I didn't know if she hadn't started to drink or if it had been refilled and how many times. I didn't care except that I wanted no more scenes with her. She was difficult enough sober; drunk, she could be obnoxious.

I wondered if the other members of the family were aware she'd followed Doug and me and if so, what she'd told them. Slowly, a feeling of resentment filled me as I thought of the man who'd shadowed us. Even if the family had hired him with the fear of kidnapping in mind, I resented it. I wanted to confront them with the fact that I was aware of what they had done. I wanted to know if they would deny it. I wanted to ask Nancy why she'd followed us, but I remembered Doug's final words of caution and I'd abide by them. Their motives could well be honorable. Nancy's, I wasn't so sure of.

I also wondered about Doug Lansing. I didn't question my love for him, but I wondered if he knew anything about me I didn't. Had I talked when I was semi-conscious? Had I said anything that could have given him a clue to the location of that apartment house in Santa Monica? Had he just pretended to drive in a hit-or-miss choice of streets, to finally go down the one where the apartment house I recognized was located?

Marilyn broke into my musings. "Where did you have dinner?"

"At a chalet on one of the canyon roads in Malibu. It commands a magnificent view of the ocean."

"I know the place," she said.

"Excellent food and superb service," Richie observed. "Were you in time to see the regatta?"

"Yes. And it was beautiful. The sailboats looked like toys on the water. They were stranded because the wind died down."

He smiled. "I wonder how many stuck it out."

"Most of them," I said. "Of course, once it got dark, they weren't visible. The moon was just coming up when we left."

Janet said, "Did you remember the restaurant?"

"Was I there before?" I asked.

"Several times," she said. "Luncheons mostly. With me. I like it there in mid-day. As you say, the view is breathtaking."

"When there's no fog," Nancy said, making a face.

Richie smiled tolerantly. "Don't go when there's fog."

"I don't go there any time," she replied petulantly.

Marilyn grimaced. "You only go where there's bugs crawling around in a drop of water. They give me the creeps."

"Then you should be writhing in agony," Nancy said. "Your body is full of millions of them. Take some scrapings from the gum line of your mouth and you'll find it infested with them."

Janet said, "Please, girls. I have a headache and I can't stand your bickering tonight."

Richie drank deeply of his wine. "Nancy's right though. I learned that much in college. Confidentially, it's the real reason I drink so much alcohol. The bugs can't live in the stuff."

Janet switched the conversation away from Marilyn and Nancy. "Did you have a pleasant day with the doctor, Sandra?"

"Very," I said. "He drove me around quite a bit. My eyes got tired seeking out something that had a familiar look or would make me cry out in recognition."

"No luck?" Richie asked.

"None." I looked directly at Nancy when I replied, but her features bore a bland look.

Janet appeared concerned. "I hope he isn't trying his brand of therapy on you. It might conflict with Dr. Beardsley's ideas of what's good for you."

"Doug is a general practitioner," I said. "Dr. Beardsley a psychiatrist."

"Just remember that." There was a touch of sternness in her voice which she softened with a smile. "I'm sorry if I seem possessive or bossy, Sandra, only I can't help but worry about you. Each time you leave the house I'm uneasy until you return."

"Please don't be," I said. "I feel no fear outside. The only thing that troubles me is my loss of memory. And my behavior before the accident. That *does* concern me—greatly."

Richie stood up, set his glass on the mantel and sat down on the arm of Janet's chair. He drew her to him. "I don't want you upsetting Sandra."

"I don't mean to upset her, Richie."

"I know that, darling, but you've got to stop worrying

127

about her. Her mind will straighten out eventually and she will have recall. If not total, then almost. Dr. Beardsley has assured us of that. In the meantime, you can help her most by relaxing and not exercising such close vigilance."

Janet smiled up at her husband. "You're right, of course."

Marilyn said, "I think we're all edgy tonight."

"You're edgy because your precious Sid hasn't returned from San Francisco," Nancy said.

"I suppose," Marilyn said. "I wish he'd hire someone to help him with the work connected with this estate. It's too much for one man."

"Why don't you help him?" Nancy was intent on needling her sister. Janet certainly hadn't lied about that. "If you spent less time in a beauty salon, you might improve your mind. Your body is perfect now. Goodness knows, it gets the best care."

Marilyn uncurled her legs from under her, stood up and glared down at her sister. "Why must you always be so bitchy?"

Nancy sipped her wine complacently. "I'm no more bitchy than you."

Marilyn turned to me. "A pity you had to get involved in that accident. Just before your last disappearance, you ordered Nancy from the house. That's when she made the grand tour and took the photographs of every member of the family, brought them to her lab and poured acid over them. Family group pictures, wedding pictures, christenings, school groups, every imaginable kind of picture. I marvel she spared the twins those pictures of themselves in their dancing costumes. But then, I suppose that was because she worshipped Larry."

Nancy was so startled at Marilyn's tirade that the glass slipped from her hand and dropped into her lap, spilling the liquid onto her dark dress. The material readily absorbed it, but left a dark stain. She set the unbroken glass on the hearth, stood up and slowly advanced toward Marilyn. Richie stepped between them.

"All right, girls," he said. "That's enough. You know what these scenes do to your mother."

"Gives her a migraine," Nancy said unfeelingly. "She's got pills for them."

"Please leave us," Richie said. "These sessions are becoming unbearable—even for me."

"Are you ordering me from the house?" she demanded.

"No," he replied quietly.

She turned to me. "Are you, Sandra?"

"No," I replied. I was as sick of the verbal tirade as Richie and Janet, yet I sensed Nancy was more hurt than angry.

"You don't like me though," she said. "You promised to come to my lab and look at my specimens, but you never did."

"I will tomorrow," I said.

She looked doubtful and her mouth opened to say something, then closed to a grim line. She walked from the room, her soggy dress clinging to her figure.

No one spoke until we heard the door to her room close. Then Marilyn addressed me. "Why do you want to go to her smelly old lab?"

"Because I think we should try to help her."

"Help her," Marilyn exclaimed. "How?"

"I'm not sure how," I said. "But it's difficult for her to see you looking so radiantly beautiful every day. I think it fills her with despair."

"She has the same opportunity as I," Marilyn said. "It's every woman's responsibility to make the most of what she has."

I said, "I know that, but she isn't interested in beautifying herself. She wants a little praise for the work she does in her lab. I have a feeling she'd be bored to death nurturing her vanity and when it comes down to it, I think I would be too."

Richie regarded me in surprise. "That doesn't sound like you."

"I can't help it. It's how I feel now. Apparently I've changed."

Janet said, "You have, Sandra. And I'm sorry you had to witness the scene between Nancy and Marilyn. It doesn't do you any good and Marilyn knows it."

"I'm sorry, Mother, Sandra."

I said, "I wasn't affected by it, except to feel a certain

129

sympathy toward Nancy." They regarded me with amazement. "I know it sounds ridiculous, but it's the way I feel."

Richie said, "Perhaps you can reach her in a way we never could."

I said, "I'm going to make the effort. As for now, I'm tired. Please 'excuse me."

They nodded understanding and we exchanged goodnights. I went to my suite, undressed, and lay in darkness. Long after I heard the others pass my door on the way to their rooms, my mind attempted vainly to answer the myriad questions which crowded it. But my efforts were in vain. I was certain of one thing though—I loved Douglas Lansing. I didn't know what the family would think of it when they heard the news, yet I hoped they'd hear it shortly. By that I meant that my memory would return and I'd be completely well. The mystery of my disappearances before the accident still plagued me, but I followed Doug's advice and didn't dwell on them. Tomorrow I would visit Nancy in her laboratory. I wondered if she had any special reason for wanting me to go there. I'd not worry over that problem until I was confronted by it. I had enough to think of now.

I awoke with the knowledge I'd promised to visit Nancy and I prided myself on the fact that I hadn't forgotten. After breakfast I walked out into the bright, warm day and made my way to the small building where she kept her lab.

She was wearing a chemical-stained smock, her hair was awry and she had no make-up on, but amidst these things she loved, she looked very much at ease and quite attractive. She regarded me with surprise.

"You meant it when you said you'd come."

"Of course I did. You know, Nancy, when you're feeling at ease with yourself, doing what you like to do, you're a very pretty girl."

She looked pleased. "Thank you, Sandy. Nobody ever said that to me before."

"Maybe you never gave them the chance," I said.

"Maybe," she agreed. "I wouldn't believe them anyway. Besides, Marilyn's right. I'd rather talk about a colpoda."

"What's a colpoda?"

"It's a tiny protozoan. An animal, a one-celled creature who is born, lives a few hours and dies. Just as we do. They look like a lima bean and they can swim a thousand times faster than any Olympic star. I can show you some of them. That is . . . if you're interested."

"I'm interested, Nancy. Please let me see one of those creatures."

She quickly and expertly prepared a slide, covered the drop of water with a coverslip, placed it under the lens, and focused for me.

"The water is alive with them. I took this lot from what we call a clone. That means I segregated a single colpoda, put him alone in a special container and fed him. He multiplied by splitting in half until there were thousands of them in that small jar. They all came from one individual. They move fast, but you'll be able to recognize them easily."

I bent over the microscope. I knew how to use one apparently, because my hand reached for the fine focusing dial. The tiny, microscopical animals came into view. They darted about wildly, bumping into one another without injury; they congregated around small masses of substance which Nancy informed me were colonies of bacteria upon which the colpoda fed.

"What I want to do—my ambition," she said after I straightened up, "is to get some of these on slides and freeze them there so nothing is changed, so they can be seen in detail. It's very hard to do, but I'm going to develop a way and when I succeed I'll turn to other protozoans." She waved a hand at a row of bottles half filled with water of varying shades and substances. "I've got them by the millions."

"And these prepared slides will help students of protozoology to study these creatures?"

"There are slides of them, but none are much good. So many details are lost."

"I'm proud of you," I said. "I don't know how dependent you are on the family money, but so long as I handle it, you may buy anything you need to help you get the results you want. There's no limit to what you may spend."

She looked astounded. "Tell Sid, will you? He doesn't

like doling out money for this. He calls it a waste. But it's not. It will do some good, honestly."

"Of course it will. I'll tell him to pay any bill you incur. On one condition."

There must have been many conditions in her life, for her face fell.

I said, "You've got to let me know of your progress. I want to come here and help. You can teach me the techniques of this work, if you have the time."

Her hand reached out and caught mine. "I don't know what to say. I don't know how to say 'thank you' in the way I should. I may sound conceited, but you've made me feel I can do whatever I want to do."

"Just what do you want to do?"

"I want to teach."

"What's stopping you if you have your degrees?"

"I have them, but mother refuses to permit it."

I couldn't repress a smile. "Why didn't you rebel?"

"I know what you mean." A note of resentment crept into her voice. "You've seen me at my worst. You think I'm like that all the time."

"Are you like that because you've not been permitted to teach?"

She paused a moment before answering. "No."

"Is it Marilyn?"

"She likes to needle me."

"You told me I also needled you."

"*You* don't. *You* aren't mean."

"What do you mean *I* don't?"

Again she hesitated. "I don't know what I mean. I guess I'm as confused in my mind as you are in yours. I'm sorry, Sandra. You're not confused. You just can't remember. That puts me at an advantage because you don't know if I'm telling you the truth or lying to you."

"Have you lied to me?"

She bit at her lower lip and turned away. "Yes. But I guess my mother told you I'm a liar."

"She said you made up stories."

She nodded. Only the back of her head was visible so I had no idea of what was going through her mind. I already realized her face reflected the inner workings of her mind. I sensed she wanted to tell me something, yet couldn't bring herself to do so. Did she want to confess she'd spied on Doug and me yesterday? I didn't wish to confront her with the fact that I'd seen her, lest I destroy the beginning of a friendship. And so I said nothing.

"I'm going to help you get that teaching job, Nancy," I said.

She spun around. "You mean it?"

"I mean it."

"I'll be ever grateful."

"I must go back to the house now. I'll see you later."

I wanted to call Doug's office and I also wanted to see Janet to tell her I'd accompany Gilbert to the school the twins attended and pick them up this afternoon.

We met in the hall. She was leaving with a small valise in each hand. They were obviously children's luggage.

Her face brightened at sight of me. "Sandra, I'm so glad I saw you. Mrs. Towers phoned. She has a daughter the same age as the twins and she asked if they might spend the night with her daughter. They're great friends. I hope you don't mind. I did check your suite to ask your permission, but you weren't there."

"I could take them," I said.

"Mrs. Towers is going to pick them up. Her daughter attends the same school, so I'm going to deliver their bags at the school. Did you wish to accompany me?"

"No." I was disappointed but tried not to show it. "I can keep busy."

"How about shopping this afternoon?"

"If you wish."

I went upstairs to my room. I knew Doug would be in his office and I felt I shouldn't call him, but I had to hear the sound of his voice. I hoped to catch him before he went out to lunch.

I dialed his number, but there was no answer. Not even the answering service picked up the phone and that was strange. I waited five minutes and tried again. This time I got the service and was told that Dr. Lansing's office was temporarily closed. I was given the name of a doctor who was taking his calls and caring for his patients.

I thanked them and hung up, completely puzzled. *Why* was his office closed? And for how long a period of time? Certainly, if he had any idea of going away, he'd have told me. Or he'd have called me here. Even if I hadn't got the call, a message would have been left. I couldn't believe his interest in me yesterday had been false; his declaration of love, feigned.

I went in search of Ethel and found her in the kitchen, discussing the dinner with Dicie. She assured me there'd been no calls, except from Mr. Sidney who had phoned Miss Marilyn. I thanked her and returned upstairs, pausing only long enough to get my purse.

I went to the garage. Gilbert, clad in hip boots, with a rubber apron covering most of him, was washing two cars.

I spoke without pausing. "I'm taking the Fiat."

"Miss Sandra, you have no license. Besides, I was told you were not to drive until you're completely well."

"I feel great, Gilbert." He'd stopped his work and stood beside the car. I was studying the unfamiliar controls.

I got it started, backed it out, turned it and headed down the drive. I could see Gilbert in the mirror, watching me, holding the hose from which water still poured, his face a study in frustration.

At least, I hadn't forgotten how to drive. Once on Sunset, I slowed my speed, for I didn't want to be stopped. Not now. I sensed something had happened to Doug. I had to find him.

FIFTEEN

The door to Doug's office was locked. I knocked several times without drawing any response. There was a dentist's office next door and the young receptionist-nurse was accommodating.

"I'm not sure what it's all about," she said, "but Dr. Lansing's nurse tore out of here like the place was on fire. That was this morning. She said something about police."

"Do you know where she lives?" I asked. "I'm a friend of Dr. Lansing."

"I'm sorry. I'm new here and I don't know his nurse too well. Maybe the police could help. Headquarters is in City Hall, unless it's the Los Angeles cops and not the Beverly Hills police. . . ."

"Thank you," I said. I returned to the street, now frantic because I knew something had happened to Doug. I asked directions and was instructed how to reach the Beverly Hills Police.

They knew nothing about Dr. Lansing, but they were most helpful. They called the Los Angeles police and I had my answer.

"Dr. Lansing was in an auto accident early this morning," the desk lieutenant told me. "He was taken to Linden Hospital. I don't know his condition. You'd better inquire there."

"Thank you," I said.

Now I had to determine where Linden Hospital was. I was told it was on Olympic near Santa Monica. I found it easily. The receptionist checked and told me that Dr. Lansing was in Room 709. I would be permitted to see him briefly, though his condition was serious.

I walked into the room to find Doug's office nurse, in uniform, caring for him. She looked up as I entered and placed a cautioning forefinger to her lips. She then led me into the corridor.

"He's unconscious and there's a fracture of the skull besides some other broken bones, but they think he has a good chance to pull through."

I controlled my emotions and asked, "What happened?"

"The police say a car was reported off one of the mountain roads. It was Dr. Lansing's car and he was in the wreckage. They pried him loose and got him here as quickly as possible. The police said it was evident that his car was hit broadside and sent crashing over the edge of the cliff. They believe it was done deliberately. They're looking for the car that was responsible."

"When did it happen?"

"Last night. Or rather, early morning before daylight. I'm going to stay with him. I'm an R.N."

"What is your name?"

"Grace Arnold. You're Mrs. Larrabee."

"Then you're aware that I can afford to see that everything is done for Dr. Lansing that can be done. Will you see to it?"

"I will, Mrs. Larrabee. Thanks."

"Do you know what he was doing on a mountain road early in the morning?"

"The police say they found a slip of paper in the car with the doctor's handwriting on it. The paper had an address. Apparently he'd had an emergency call. He's the kind of doctor who will go out at any hour. But the police say the address was nonexistent."

136

"Do you know of any reason why someone would wish to kill him?" I asked.

"Absolutely none, Mrs. Larrabee."

"Someone does," I said. "Is there any indication when he'll wake up?"

"No. It may be several days, or he might open his eyes in the next ten minutes. The fracture has been repaired, there's no permanent brain damage that they have determined so far. His vital signs are good, considering what he's going through."

I wrote down my phone number. "Please—if he does no more than open his eyes, call me at once."

She slipped the number into the pocket of her uniform. "I'll do it the moment he wakes up."

"Is the doctor in charge of his case in the hospital?"

"Yes. He was doing several operations today. You might find him in the doctor's lounge. His name is Tracy."

"Thank you," I said. "I may be back in a few minutes. Depends on what Dr. Tracy tells me."

I located the lounge, but Dr. Tracy was still in surgery, though he was expected to come out soon. The floor nurse promised to tell him I was waiting. I sat down, grateful for a few moments in which to rest and think and, most of all, plan.

It was evident to me that the attack on Doug had been made because he was helping me. Someone was frightened, but why? Was that the reason the man had been shadowing us yesterday? Could Nancy be aware of what had happened to him and the reason for it—or was she directly involved? She must have followed us also. Somebody feared Doug. Did he know something I didn't? Was someone fearful I'd regain my memory? Did I present a menace to that person if I should? But why? And who? I didn't know. The answers didn't come and I didn't want to point the finger of guilt at Nancy without proof. And a mere glimpse of her at the apartment house that struck a familiar chord in my mind was not enough to accuse her of attempted murder.

In my opinion, Doug was still in mortal danger. Whoever tried to kill him would likely know by now that the attempt had been a failure and another attack might be made. The thought terrified me, but I knew what I was

137

going to do. I left the lounge to make my way to a phone booth just down the corridor. The glass booth was situated so I had a view of the doctors' lounge.

I called St. Bartholomew Hospital and asked for Mildred Brewster, charge nurse on the floor where I'd been a patient for such a long time.

"Millie," I said, "this is Sandra Larrabee. I wish a favor from you. Is the large private room that was next to mine available?"

"Yes," she said. "Patient left an hour ago. What's the matter? Are you feeling bad again?"

"No . . . no. A friend of mine has been in an auto accident and is seriously hurt. He's unconscious at the moment and I have to find out if he can be safely moved. I want him at St. Bartholomew's because I know the hospital and you . . . and the others on the floor so well."

"We'll take good care of your friend if he is sent here," she assured me.

"Good. As soon as I find out, I'll give you more details. You've no idea how pleased I am by your cooperation. And reserve the room now. Give my name."

"Okay, Mrs. Larrabee. Count on us."

I returned to the lounge and had to wait another twenty minutes before a doctor emerged from the surgeon's dressing rooms. He was middle-aged and his features were drawn with fatigue. He stepped into the lounge.

"Are you Dr. Tracy?" I asked.

"Yes. May I help you?"

"I'm a friend of Dr. Lansing."

"Oh yes. Well, I'm sure he'll do. I can't say when he'll regain consciousness. He had a severe knock on the head. He's very lucky to be alive."

"I know you've done your best for him and I'm grateful. Now I wish to know if he can be safely moved to another hospital."

"Yes, but what's the matter with this one?"

"Nothing, but I have important reasons for wanting him admitted to St. Bartholomew's."

"That's no problem. I'm on staff there also. Before giving him a release, I'll look in on him to make sure."

"Thank you, Doctor."

We walked down the corridor to Doug's room. "Are you related to him?" Dr. Tracy asked.

"No. We met at St. Bartholomew's while I was a patient there. I was struck by a car."

Dr. Tracy looked apprehensive. "I thought you were a relative."

"I hope to be—shortly. We plan to be married. My name is Sandra Larrabee."

"Oh." He eyed me with greater interest. "I remember. You're the Larrabee heiress."

"So they tell me. I have amnesia, you know. Or did you?"

"I seem to recall some talk of it at the hospital. Well, Miss Larrabee, I'll check my patient and if I feel he can be moved, I'll give the order and also have him checked in at St. Bartholomew's."

"Thank you, Doctor. And it's Mrs. Larrabee—I'm Larry Larrabee's widow."

He nodded. "That's right. I forgot."

We reached the room and Dr. Tracy went in, closing the door behind him. He was there about ten minutes. When he came out, he said, "He can be moved. I'll take care of it immediately."

"I'm sure Doug won't be offended if I assume all expenses."

"He's in no position to, Mrs. Larrabee, and under the circumstances I feel he'd have no objection."

I asked Grace to accompany Doug in the ambulance and she agreed. I'd follow in the Fiat. I told her then why I was transferring him to St. Bartholomew's. "Like the police, I don't believe it was an accident and feel he'll be safer there since I know the nurses and hospital help. And I'll ask Dr. Tracy to get assurances that only authorized personnel will be permitted to enter his room. I know you'll cooperate."

"I will, Mrs. Larrabee. Will you have other specials for him?"

"I'm going to ask Dr. Tracy to order them. I don't want him left alone for a moment."

"Are you saying that whoever tried to murder Dr. Lansing might try again?"

"Yes."

She looked apprehensive.

"Would you rather not be on the case?" I asked.

"Oh, I want to be," she said. "I just can't imagine who would do such a thing."

"I can't either," I said. "That's why we must exercise such caution."

She went back into the room. Dr. Tracy was just hanging up the telephone when I passed the floor desk. I informed him of the precautions I wanted him to take, and why.

He said, "I'm going to St. Bartholomew's now. I'll talk with them and order two more specials for him. They'll be told that if they should have to leave the room for any purpose, someone on the floor is to remain with him until they return."

"Thank you, Doctor. I appreciate your cooperation. Just do everything possible to make him well."

"Once he regains consciousness, you'll be able to do more than any of us."

"Thank you, Doctor. I'll be at his side."

Dr. Tracy left me and I waited until a stretcher came to take Doug. I accompanied Grace to the ambulance. Before I got my car, I telephoned St. Bartholomew's and talked to the charge nurse again. I was assured Dr. Tracy had made all arrangements and they were waiting for the patient. The transfer was made efficiently. At St. Bartholomew's the hospital administrator told me the door would not only be closed, but guarded from the inside by the installation of a stout chain.

I stayed at the hospital until word came that Doug had not suffered in the least by his transfer. His pulse was getting stronger and there were indications he would wake up sooner than they'd expected. I felt a slight sense of relief and I left the hospital. There was a great deal to do and, at last, I had a certain course to follow. Doug had set it up. Now it was my duty to see that I explored all the avenues. Somewhere, in one of the darker ones, I'd find out what this was all about. At the moment, I didn't have the slightest idea.

I drove to Santa Monica and located the apartment house Doug and I had visited. I parked and walked slowly toward the entrance. More and more, I had a feeling I'd been here often in the past. I knew that two blocks south was a supermarket, and there were a number of small shops along the boulevard. True, I might have seen them during Doug's driving about, but I thought these stores were more in my memory—my past—rather than my present. I walked into the patio, hoping I wouldn't run into the manager. I rang the bell of the first apartment I came to.

An elderly woman answered. "I'm sorry to bother you," I said. "I'm trying to get some information. A friend of mine used to live here, but the manager doesn't seem to know where she's gone."

"Don't even bother to give me her name," the woman said. "Come in. You don't look like a saleswoman trying to peddle something."

I entered a spacious, tastefully furnished living room. The woman immediately explained. "I asked you in because the manager has long ears. He's always snooping. Now, what did you wish to know? Oh yes . . . a friend of yours lived here. Well, I don't think anybody in this apartment house can enlighten you about her. You see, a few months ago, this corner was to be turned into a high-rise office complex and the apartment house was sold. Everyone living here was asked to leave and paid well if leases had to be broken. Then it was discovered the property wasn't suited, maybe because of zoning. I don't know. Anyway, it was up for rent again and it filled up real fast. Nobody, including the manager, has been here more than two months."

"I see. Well, I'll try elsewhere. Thank you very much."

"The only thing left from the old tenants is the car in the garage. That was here when I moved in. I was the first one, you see. The manager said it was his car, but I don't believe him. He's got one he leaves on the street and this one in the garage is covered with tarp so you can't even see the bumpers."

"Thank you again," I said.

I left and returned to the street, but the idea of a car having been left in the garage after the previous tenants all moved away, intrigued me.

I knew where the garage entrance was located and I paused to look about before I entered. It was dimly lighted

141

and gloomy even in full daylight. At the far end of the garage and close to the wall was the covered automobile. I didn't have the key that had been in my old handbag. Doug was the last to have it and I wondered if it had been among his possessions.

I lifted the dusty cover enough to determine that this was a Chevrolet. I dropped the cover, raised it again at the rear of the vehicle and noted the marker number. Then I hurried out before I was caught snooping about.

I drove down the street, turned left and headed for Los Angeles. Traffic was heavy, for it was now late afternoon. They'd be worried about me at home, but I paid little heed to that. They were entitled to an explanation and I intended to give them one.

A traffic light flashed red and I stopped rather short. My front wheels were just over the cross walk. To my right, a high-rise insurance company building was disgorging its workers. They were mostly office girls. One of them, a tall brunette in a white blouse and red skirt, gave me a cursory glance and turned away. As quickly, her head pivoted back and her face broke into a broad smile.

"Liz," she called, certainly to me, "Liz, long time no see. Call me."

I automatically raised my hand in a signal I understood. I wanted to stop her, to question her, but at that moment the light changed, the cars behind me blew their horns to express their resentment at my slow start. I had to drive on for two blocks before I found a parking space. I got out, ran back, but my search of the whole area was fruitless. Whoever the girl was, she'd vanished.

Liz! Elizabeth! It was too common a name to test for familiarity. Anyway, I was Sandra Larrabee. The girl must have mistaken me for this Liz, whoever she was. Unless I had used a false name during my disappearances? I returned to my car and before I started it, I wrote down the number of the Chevrolet that was parked in the garage and covered with tarpaulin.

I stopped at the hospital. The charge nurse on the early evening shift signaled that all was well. I knocked softly on the door to Doug's room. Grace opened the door a crack, closed it again to slip the chain and let me in. The chain went back on immediately.

The resident was there and when Grace introduced me, he said, "Dr. Lansing is responding well. We expect him to come out of it within twenty-four hours. He's no longer in any danger."

"Has anyone tried to see him?" I asked.

"Who knows he's here?" Grace asked. "But if anybody comes, we're ready."

"No one will get in," the resident assured me. "Bank on it. I'm staying with him as much as possible."

I said, "I think Dr. Lansing's life may depend on it. Thank you."

Grace let me out and I drove directly home. Janet, Richie, and Sid, who'd returned from San Francisco, were waiting for me in the drawing room. Their concerned faces relaxed at sight of me.

Janet said, "Thank God you're back." "Whatever possessed you to take a car—which you're not supposed to do, and certainly not without a license?"

"I'm afraid I didn't really care about the license."

Sid said, "I don't suppose you had the slightest bit of identification on you."

"That's something I didn't think of," I admitted.

"And suppose you'd been stopped by the police," he went on.

"I wasn't," I said complacently.

"No, dear, you weren't," Janet agreed. "But you mustn't be irritated because we were at our wit's end worrying about you."

"I don't want you to worry about me," I said. "Besides, Janet, I'll not be babied."

"It isn't that," she said. "Our fear is that you'll disappear again and this time we won't be able to find you."

"Such a thought never occurred to me. I wanted a car and I took it."

"We know that." Richie spoke as he poured himself a drink from a crystal decanter. "What concerned us was that Gilbert said you were highly agitated."

"That's true," I agreed.

"About what?" he asked.

Before I could answer, Marilyn entered the room. "What a relief to see you. May I have my bracelet back?"

"Bracelet?" I regarded my wrists. I wasn't even wearing a watch, nor had I even thought about one.

"You took it from my room," she said.

"No, I didn't, Marilyn," I said.

"Ethel saw you coming out of there. She said you were carrying a diamond bracelet. I queried the servants today after I found it missing."

I said, "I'll admit I was in your suite. I don't recall appropriating the bracelet. Certainly I'm not wearing it."

She said, "It's not in the safe. I checked. I don't like mentioning it since you've been so generous about everything, including loaning your jewelry to Mother and me whenever we expressed a desire to borrow it."

"I'm glad you mentioned it," I said. "I'll check my rooms and see if I did absentmindedly pick it up and place it in one of the drawers."

Sid smiled self-consciously. "It's not in a class with yours, but for Marilyn, it has a sentimental value. I gave it to her."

"I hope I haven't turned into a kleptomaniac as well as an amnesiac."

"Our concern is for you, my dear," Janet said. "Not the missing bracelet."

Marilyn said, "I don't want to make an issue of the missing bracelet, but I'd like to know what happened to it."

"So would I," I said. "Particularly since Ethel saw me with it."

"She didn't say the bracelet you carried was mine," Marilyn said. "Just that you were carrying a diamond bracelet. Mother questioned the other servants, but they know nothing about it. Ava is the only maid who works upstairs."

"She came highly recommended," Janet said.

Richie finished his drink and got up to refill the glass. "That doesn't mean too much nowadays."

"I'm sure Ava wouldn't take it," I said. "She seems quite happy here and is wonderful with the twins."

Richie said, "Oh, to hell with the bracelet. I want to know what happened to upset you so you'd take a car when you have no license. Also, when Dr. Beardsley told us in no uncertain terms you were not to drive."

144

"I learned Doug Lansing was injured in an auto accident."

Janet said, "I'm very sorry to hear it. Is he seriously injured?"

"Yes," I replied. "He was taken to Linden Hospital. That's where I went. He's unconscious, but I checked with his doctor and asked if he could be moved. I wanted him at St. Bartholomew's because I'm familiar with it. Dr. Tracy gave his permission and the transfer was made. He's there now."

Marilyn said, "No wonder you're so pale."

Janet said, "When did you eat last?"

"Breakfast, I guess," I said. "I'm not hungry."

Richie said, "You won't help yourself by not eating."

"I know," I admitted. "I'll have a tray in my room if Ethel doesn't mind."

"You're tired, aren't you?" Janet was eying me with concern.

"A little. But also relieved." I turned to Sid. "Please draw a check for one hundred thousand dollars payable to St. Bartholomew's Hospital as a gift. I'd like it done tomorrow."

"One hundred thousand?" Sid's face was tinged with disbelief.

Richie said, "It almost sounds as if you're bribing St. Bartholomew to give Dr. Lansing special care."

"Nothing of the kind," I replied. "And I'm certain under such circumstances, they'd not accept it. It's because they gave me such excellent care even before they knew who I was or who was going to pay the bill."

Janet said, "But don't you think that's excessive, dear?"

"No. In any case, it's the amount I wish to donate."

Sid said, "I'll take care of it tomorrow. I'll have to juggle some funds to get that much in the checking account, but it will be done."

"Where's Nancy?" For the first time, I became aware of her absence from the group.

"She has one of her migraine headaches," Janet said.

"Small wonder," Marilyn said coolly. "Anyone who peers through a microscope as much as she, is bound to get headaches."

"Be fair, Marilyn," Richie said. "Nancy has suffered from them since adolescence."

"I know," Marilyn said. "But why won't she help herself?"

"Won't she see a doctor about them?" I asked.

Janet said, "It's her personality that's mostly to blame. Dr. Beardsley has tried to treat her, but she ridicules his efforts. That is, at the house. She won't go to his office. He worked such a miracle with you, I invited him here while you were still in the hospital, in the hope he could reach Nancy. Thus far, his efforts have been in vain."

Richie said, "Nancy is too obsessed with her laboratory."

I said, "I think the fault is not so much Nancy's as yours."

Janet eyed me in shocked amazement. "I don't understand."

"Nancy loves her field and wants to teach. Why not praise her work and help her do what she wants? She's rebelling against you and I feel she has every right."

"Sandra, you've never talked like this before," Janet said.

"You told me I'd changed," I said. "Nancy also told me I had. I believe she's actually beginning to like me. I hope so. At any rate, I'm going to help her get a teaching job. When she does, I'm certain her migraines will disappear and you'll have no need of Dr. Beardsley. She needs nothing more than understanding."

Richie looked thoughtful. "It could be you're right."

"I know I'm right," I said.

Marilyn said, "I'm for any change for the better in Nancy."

Sid said, "I'll second that."

Janet sighed. "It's certainly worth a try."

I felt relieved I'd won them over. "Please excuse me. I'm very tired."

Janet gave me an understanding nod. "I'll send Ethel up with a tray."

"Thank you, Janet."

I bade them good night, went upstairs and tapped on Nancy's door. It would take only a minute to tell her I knew there'd be no further opposition to her desire to teach the subject she was so wrapped up in. There was no answer. I turned the knob and looked in. Her bed lamp was on its lowest wattage and she was in bed, covered and sleeping soundly. I withdrew quietly and went to my own suite. The news would keep.

I undressed and drew a warm tub. While I was in it, I heard my door opened. Ethel called softly that she had placed a tray on the table in the sitting room. I thanked her and heard the door close again.

I toweled myself briskly, donned a nightie and robe and headed for the food which awaited me. There was a sizzling steak, along with a vegetable, salad, hot roll, ice cream and coffee.

I ate most of it, set the tray outside my door and got into bed. I used the phone at my bedside to call the hospital and learn whether there was any change in Doug's condition. I was informed there wasn't and worried about it, wondering if that was a favorable or unfavorable sign.

But I was also exhausted from the tenseness of the day and fell asleep wondering who had lured him to a mountain road and there sent him hurtling off the cliff in his car. I hoped when he awakened, he'd have the answer.

I must have been deep in sleep when the noises began, for I awakened to them slowly. It sounded to me like people struggling. Once I heard a brief cry. Not a scream, but a sharp cry as if from pain and I thought it was a woman's voice.

I got out of bed quickly, but before I got into my robe and slippers I heard the front door close and a minute later a car pulled away from in front of the house. I left my suite and headed for the stairs. Ethel was on her way up, her face grim.

"What happened?" I asked.

"It was Ava—the upstairs maid. She came in my room and woke me up. She was drunk and was wearing Miss Marilyn's bracelet."

"You mean she stole it?"

"Must've. The family didn't want to tell you, Miss Sandra. But other things have been missing from the house —also a fair sum of money. I called the garage and Gilbert came. Took the two of us to bring her downstairs to the car. He brought her home. I'm going to pack her bag now and he can bring it to her in the morning."

"I heard her cry out as if in pain."

"That was me, Miss Sandra. She kicked me in the ankle. Sorry I woke you."

I returned to my room, still troubled by the disturbance. Sleep came, but not soon. I made another call to the hospital and received the same disappointing report, though I took consolation in the fact that Doug's condition hadn't worsened.

SIXTEEN

The first thing I did upon awakening was to phone the hospital. It was a few minutes after seven and I knew Grace would be there. Her cautious manner changed to one of warmth when she recognized my voice.

She said, "I already talked with the resident who gave me the good news that Dr. Lansing wakened before I came on duty. He asked a couple of questions. Naturally the effort tired him, but I knew you'd be as pleased to hear it as I was when I came on duty."

"I am," I said. "How is he now?"

"Sleeping, but he's beginning to stir. He's probably waking up again."

"If he does, ask him to please rest until I get there—which will be as fast as I can make it."

I showered and dressed hastily. I didn't want to delay my departure even for breakfast, but I had many things I wanted to do today and I knew I'd probably not take time again to eat. I was glad no one was in the dining room when I came down. Dicie brought my breakfast, a puffy omelet, along with country sausage. It would fortify me until I returned.

I'd brought my purse downstairs with me and after a few sips of coffee, I left the house and went to the garage. Gilbert didn't even look surprised when I got into the Fiat, waved a farewell, and headed down the drive. I could read his mind though. He'd given me no argument and I imagined he was thinking since he'd reported to the family what I'd done, it was no longer his affair. I agreed. I knew I was doing wrong in driving without a license, but I felt the circumstances warranted it. At least, that was the excuse I used, though perhaps not a just one.

At the hospital, I took the elevator to Doug's room and was walking briskly along the corridor when I heard my name called. I turned to see Dr. Beardsley striding toward me, a welcoming smile on his face.

"Were you looking for me, Sandra?" he asked.

I returned the smile. "Do I look as if I need a doctor?"

He sobered. "No, you don't. I was wondering if the family had tried to get me. I was up with a sick patient most of the night and I haven't checked with my answering service to see if I had any calls. When I spotted you I thought you needed me and decided to seek me out."

"No, Doctor."

"How's Nancy?"

"I didn't see her last night when I returned after a day's outing. I was told she had a headache."

"I hope that's all it is," he said, sobering.

"What do you mean?"

"I'm not sure," he said. "I only hope she's not headed for a breakdown. She lives in that laboratory, you know."

I nodded. "It's her sanctuary."

"What do you mean?"

"You know how wrapped up she is in protozoology. She's also frustrated because Janet won't let her teach."

"Her mother feels that there's no need for her to do so, and, in all fairness, there isn't."

"No, except that she'll be doing something worthwhile and that's what she wants."

"I agree," he said. "Why don't you speak to Mrs. Larrabee about it?"

"I already have and believe I've won them over."

"Good." His features relaxed in a smile. But as quickly,

150

he resumed his professional look. "Then why are you here, Sandra?"

"Dr. Lansing is a patient here."

"What's wrong with him?"

"He was in a motor accident. His car was hit broadside on a canyon road and fell several feet. He was severely injured."

"I'm sorry to hear it. Tell him if there's anything I can do, I'll be glad to."

"Thank you, Doctor, but his prognosis is good. Dr. Tracy is handling the case."

Dr. Beardsley nodded assurance. "One of the best. I'll drop in and say hello to your doctor later."

"I'm afraid you'll find a no-visitor sign on his door. When he's feeling better, I'll be glad to have you stop by. Just now I want him to do nothing but rest. I'm the only visitor allowed."

He gave me a knowing look. "So it's serious between the two of you."

I nodded. "Very. That's why I'm here."

Dr. Beardsley patted my arm lightly. "Good girl. The sight of you will do more for him than any doctor."

I thanked him and continued on to Doug's room. I knocked lightly on the door. Grace opened it a few inches, nodded at me, then closed it to slide the chain free. The head of Doug's bed was raised slightly. His eyes were open and at sight of me, he managed a smile.

I said, "How are you, darling?"

"A little groggy, but coming out of it fast."

"I know Dr. Tracy is pleased. So am I."

"Grace told me I was taken to Linden and you had me transferred here." His glance shifted to Grace, now standing beside the bed. "Why don't you relax with a cup of coffee?"

She laughed. "In other words, take a walk. I will if Mrs. Larrabee will put the chain on the door after I leave."

"Thanks, Grace." I walked with her to the door.

"Don't let him talk too much," she cautioned. "He needs rest and plenty of it."

"I know. And thanks for being so understanding."

"I like my doctor and I like the girl he's in love with,"

151

she said, her smile warm. "You're good therapy for him."

After she went out, I slid the chain in place and returned to Doug's bedside.

"I was just warned I'm not to tire you."

"A few things I have to say. After that, I'll rest." His voice was weak and the words came hesitantly. His hand reached for mine and closed around it. "I love you, Sandra."

"And I love you. If you're willing to accept me as I am, I won't fight it. I need you."

"You mean you could love this botched-up guy?"

I bent and kissed him lightly on the mouth. "More than ever. Dr. Tracy is pleased with your progress."

"I'm disgusted I wasn't more alert. I didn't expect anyone would make an attack on my life."

"Then you know it was deliberate."

He nodded. "The moment the car headed for me, I knew I hadn't got the address wrong and the sick call was a phony. My last conscious thought was of you and the fear you'd be next."

"If only I could think of who could be behind it."

"I thought of Nancy. You saw her at the apartment house," he said.

"Yes," I admitted. "When I returned to the house last night, everyone was in the drawing room except her. They said she had a migraine and went to bed. I talked them into letting her teach and stopped by her room later to tell her so. She was sleeping soundly or pretended to be."

"Who knew we were going to be together?"

"The whole family. But what's their motive?"

"I think I know," he said. "In fact, I know I do— if not their motive, at least why they're keeping an eye on you."

"Please tell me."

"Before I do, did you go back to that apartment house in Santa Monica?"

"Yes. I talked to one of the tenants. She told me no tenant in the building has been there longer than two months. Neither has the manager, despite what he claimed."

He pursed his lips in a soundless whistle to indicate

his surprise. I explained why the building had been vacated, then went on with my description of what I'd learned.

"This tenant also told me the only thing in the building when she moved in, was a car in the garage which was completely covered. The manager said it was his, but he owns a car that he keeps on the street, not in the garage. So I went to the garage and had myself a look. The car is a Chevrolet sedan. I took down the number, but I haven't checked it yet. I wonder if the car key found in my handbag will fit that car."

"Sure it will," he managed to say.

"Another strange thing happened. As I drove back to Los Angeles from Santa Monica, I stopped for a traffic light. There was an office building disgorging employees. One of the girls crossing in front of my car seemed to recognize me. She waved and called me Liz, and said she hadn't seen me in a long time and I was to call her."

"Did you recognize her?"

"No. She was a complete stranger to me, but she certainly knew me. She wasn't making any mistake, though Liz is a far cry from Sandra."

"Going to talk," he said in his low, almost whispering voice. "Don't ask me to stop. I know what I'm saying. My mind is clear. You have to understand that."

"I understand, darling."

"You are not Sandra Larrabee," he said.

"How can you say that?" I asked after a stunned moment.

"The twins."

"What about them?"

"When you were brought into the hospital, we did a complete physical on you. Had to. We didn't know how much damage had been done. You never gave birth to those twins or any child. You're a virgin."

Fortunately, there was a chair beside the bed, for the shock of what I'd just heard made me feel giddy. After I was seated, I said, "Is that why I couldn't feel any rapport with the twins?"

"Not necessarily. You told me how you remembered where the playroom was that Larry Larrabee used as a child. You knew the door to Janet's suite. You placed

153

your purse in a drawer you habitually used for that purpose."

"Do you know who I am?"

"I think I do. I believe also the girl who called your name recognized you, and your first name must be Elizabeth. Check the marker plates on the car in the garage at that apartment house."

"I will. When did you know I was not Sandra Larrabee?"

His answer came after a few moments of thought. "When I returned to the hospital and was told who you were, I was puzzled to learn you were a widow. When I crashed the dinner party and saw you moving about with the twins and was told they were yours, I knew for a certainty there was something wrong. That it was impossible for you to be the mother of those twins—or any child."

"Why didn't you tell me?" I asked.

"Forgive me, but I didn't know if you were playing a game. I know now you're a pawn in some kind of game the Larrabees are playing. At least, one of them is guilty. But I'd say the lot of them are. Please don't go back."

"But if I'm not Sandra Larrabee—and I'm convinced now I'm not—where is she?"

"Probably dead. That's why—you must not go back."

"They don't know what you've told me. I'm safe until they do."

"You're not safe. We . . . were . . . followed. Proves they . . . don't . . . trust you. And remember what . . . happened to . . . me." His eyes started to close.

"Go to sleep, darling. Rest. I'll sit here."

"Promise?"

I patted his hand reassuringly, moved my chair away from the bedside and sat down again. My mind was whirling. I was not a mother, not a wife. Nor had I ever been. My name was Liz Something-or-other. I had no idea why I was being passed off as Sandra Larrabee nor could I imagine which Larrabee had arranged this.

The fact that they'd tried to kill Doug indicated the extent of the seriousness with which they regarded his efforts to identify me. There was so much I wanted to

154

ask him, to discuss with him, but it would have to wait. Whatever I did now would have to be on my own.

I tried to think about reasons for this strange situation, but none would come to my mind. I then tried to think back as to who I was. I must have been in that apartment house before. I knew things about the neighborhood, indicating I had undoubtedly lived there at one time. Perhaps recently, because of the set of keys in my purse when I was found.

The accident which had sent me to the hospital had not been a deliberately planned one as was the case with Doug's, so I could find no answer there. It must lie in the Larrabee mansion, where I'd been taken and given the identity of Sandra Larrabee.

No doubt money was involved. With so much of it in the fortune the genuine Sandra had inherited, money had to have something to do with this situation. Therefore, money was the weak point in their defense. I must prevent whoever was responsible from reaping a profit by this deception. Only then would I be safe. I set about trying to think of a way to do this. I had a feeling that in the past I'd handled my own affairs boldly and I had faith I could do so again. But how?

I was deep in thought when a light tap sounded on the door. I checked before slipping the chain free and was relieved to see it was Grace. She went to Doug's bedside immediately, put a thermometer between his lips, attached a blood pressure cuff and checked his pulse. Her features were noncommittal, but I remained quiet until she filled out his chart.

"He's in good shape now. There's an ankle fracture, not too severe. And he's got two badly skinned knees, a severely bruised hip and some nearly fractured ribs. Nothing there that won't heal fast. Especially if you're here to hold his hand."

"I may not be all the time, Grace. There's a great deal for me to do. But I'll be here as often as I can and stay as long as possible. If I'm gone when he wakes up, will you tell him that, please?"

"Of course. Believe me, there's no longer anything to worry about."

I nodded agreement, knowing Doug and I had a great

deal to worry about. Another tap on the door, though it was discreet, startled me. I opened it the length of the chain. It was Dr. Beardsley.

"How is he, my dear?"

"Asleep," I said.

"Good. Rest is the important thing. May I talk with you for a few minutes?"

"Can't it wait, Doctor?"

"It concerns Nancy. You expressed an interest in her, but if you're too busy. . . ."

"Oh no. I'll see you in the lounge."

"Thank you, Sandra."

I told Grace where I'd be, slipped the chain free of the door and closed it behind me. But I stood there until I heard her slip the chain back in place.

I headed for the lounge when the thought occurred to me that I had had no right to order Sid to donate the large sum of money to the hospital. I was not Sandra Larrabee. I wondered if he had complied. I doubted it. Certainly he must be a part of the deceit the family was practicing on me and on their friends—and also the bank. Yet where was Sandra Larrabee? And if, as Doug said, she was probably dead, had she been murdered? Had the Larrabees been forced to do away with her? For what reason?

Dr. Beardsley was pacing the floor of the spacious and comfortably furnished lounge. He led me to a chair and sat down on a settee facing me—and the morning sun which made him blink slightly.

"First of all, I want to thank you for the large diamond ring the Larrabees presented to me."

"It's the first I knew of it," I replied.

"Yet you don't seem surprised," he said.

"There've been too many surprises for me to even blink at news of another."

"I know what you're thinking," he said, smiling. "That it was your money that paid for it."

I didn't return the smile. "Such a thought never occurred to me because it wasn't my money."

His brows raised in puzzlement. "Not your money?"

"I inherited it," I said, wondering if he was a part of the game the Larrabees were playing. "I feel the twins

156

have far more right to it than I. I merely married into the family while they are true Larrabees."

He nodded. "Nonetheless, I feel embarrassed at accepting it."

"Please don't. I'm sure you've earned it."

"Not with you, Sandra. You haven't regained your memory."

"No, but I haven't given up and I hope you haven't given up on me."

"Indeed not." He regarded the diamond whose facets caught the morning sun and deluged the walls with shafts of vari-colored lights. He raised his hand so the stone was flashing in my face. Yet I didn't flinch from the flashing lights. Instead, my eyes followed it, seemingly fascinated by it. At the same time, I wished he'd get on with his reason for asking me out here.

"Sandra," he spoke sharply, "you're daydreaming."

"I'm sorry, Doctor. The ring seemed to hold me spellbound." I blinked a few times. "I'm all right now. You said you wished to talk with me about Nancy."

"Did you see her this morning?" he asked.

"I saw only the maid who served me breakfast—and I saw Gilbert when I went to the garage."

"I received a call from Janet about five minutes ago. She asked me to come at once. That Nancy is incoherent and is having crying spells."

I was startled by the news. "What could have happened?"

"I don't know. I'm going out there immediately. I wondered if you might have seen her. Or if she was normal when you left."

"I can't help you, Doctor. I'm sorry. Truly sorry."

He stood up. "So am I. I'll not keep you longer. I know you want to get back to Dr. Lansing."

I walked slowly back to the room, completely puzzled by Dr. Beardsley's behavior. He wanted to see me about Nancy, yet his first thought was of the ring. To me, it was more than a little ostentatious, particularly for a doctor to be wearing. Yet if that was the Larrabee's taste, I had no objection—particularly since I had no right to any of the money.

I was pleased when Grace checked my knock on the

door before she slid the chain free. Doug was still sleeping quietly. She immediately returned to the bedside to take his pressure again, trying not to awaken him in the process.

I answered another knock on the door. It was a nurse, holding a small tray in her hand. On it was a small paper cup holding a single white pill.

"Is he to take it now?" I asked. "He's sleeping."

"Not until just before dinner hour. That's the order that came with it, but it's to be delivered now."

I thanked her and closed the door. I placed the paper cup containing the pill on the dresser. My handbag lay next to it. I opened the handbag and removed my gloves.

"I'm leaving, Grace," I said. "I'll be back later."

"Don't worry about him, Mrs. Larrabee, and you can be sure I'll let nobody in."

I left the hospital and returned to where my car was parked. I sat there in the parking area and thought back to my time spent in the hospital. It all began when Janet Larrabee came to the hospital and identified me as Sandra. How had they learned I was there? I'd been in that hospital for two months and, during that time, no one had inquired about me. Possibly, I thought, Dr. Beardsley had seen me there and thought he recognized me. Thought? I frowned. He was obviously closely associated with the Larrabee household. Whatever their scheme was, he could conceivably be part of it. He'd seen me, noticed that I looked like Sandra Larrabee, and set the stage for what happened afterwards. I was accepted as Sandra, even displayed at a large dinner dance and been fully accepted as Sandra. So I must look very much like her. But where was Sandra?

Everything depended upon the answer to that question. It didn't require a superior intelligence to know that behind this scheme—whatever it was—lay the Larrabee fortune. In my opinion, the whole family was involved. With the exception of the twins. It occurred to me now that they were deliberately kept out of my way.

Yet how had the twins recognized me and accepted me as their mother? And how did I know so many of the small items in the childhood room of Larry Larrabee, supposedly my late husband? Why did some parts of the mansion seem familiar to me? I wondered if it was possible that I had stumbled onto a scheme so cleverly carried out that all of these doubtful items were made possible.

I wondered, too, exactly what degree of danger I might be in. They'd tried to murder Doug, probably because they estimated he must know too much. They could take no chances so he had to be killed. That was an indication to me of how huge this plot must be and to what ends they'd go to carry it out.

Again the motive was money. There could be no other unless it was connected with the disappearance of Sandra Larrabee. Therefore, the fortune became a weapon I might be able to use. They'd presented me as Sandra Larrabee, I was accepted as such, so it would be impossible for them to call me a fraud. I was still in control of the money and it could become the lever I needed. My shield against their guile and ruthlessness.

I started the car and drove straight to the bank where I'd already been accepted as Sandra Larrabee. On the way I thought of Nancy and wondered what role she played in their game of deceit.

SEVENTEEN

This time I asked to see the vice-president in charge of this branch of the bank. My name—or the one I'd been using—was enough to get me into his office promptly and my request sent him into more activity than he'd probably exerted in months. First, he summoned another vice-president in charge of trusts, then he sent for the bank's attorney to come on the double and when these men were present, the bank closed its doors for the day, but business in the vice-president's office went on.

"What I am about to tell you must be held in the strictest confidence," I warned. "The fact is, I am dissatisfied with the way my estate has been handled."

"I hope not by the bank, Mrs. Larrabee," the vice-president said.

"The bank has performed splendidly," I said with a warm smile. "That's why I am now asking that your attorney prepare a cancellation of the power of attorney that is now held by Sidney Burwell. In its place I shall appoint this bank to handle my affairs. Mr. Burwell's authorization for anything to do with my name or my estate, is to be declared void. From this moment on, he has no longer any control over my affairs. I wish the management of my properties to be placed in the hands of this bank. Should anything happen to me, I want the bank appointed trustee of my estate and it shall then act in accordance with the last will and testament I shall write here, today, and place in a safe deposit vault to be opened by you in the event the will is needed."

The three men went into action. Secretaries were sent for, legal documents dictated and ordered to be typed immediately. While this was being done, I was given a small desk in the privacy of another office where I could write what they believed to be my will. It was, instead, a detailed document relating what had happened to me, how I had been duped and so had everyone else. I told about the attempt to kill Doug. I confessed that I was still mystified by certain elements in this gigantic fraud. How the twins recognized and accepted me; how I seemed familiar with certain parts of the mansion, without knowing why. I included the address of the apartment house where I now believed I had lived and asked that an investigation be made of its ownership. I had an idea that the Larrabee interests had purchased the house, driven out the old tenants who might have recognized me and installed new ones who would not know me in the event my memory was partially restored.

So many things were becoming clear to me as I wrote out this document. In the last sentence I wrote a line that this was a true statement of facts and my signature was attested to by witnesses.

The bank officials signed it under the delusion this was my will. I did not permit them to see any of the paragraphs I'd written. They now assigned me a safe deposit box and I turned over my key with the necessary authorization allowing them to open the box in the event I was unable to do so by reason of death, disappearance, or incapacity. I signed several documents as they were explained to me.

Now I thought I had everything in order so that the Larrabee family, or those members of it who had conducted this misrepresentation, would be unable to take any action against me without running the risk of losing everything the estate represented.

161

I left the bank late in the afternoon, with the officials mentally rubbing their hands in glee of putting over this highly profitable transaction with the least amount of effort. I felt sorry for them. There was going to be a rude and unexpected awakening.

I now drove straight back to the mansion of evil, hidden behind the respectable façade of a Sunset Boulevard estate. I drove to the garage and left the car outside. Gilbert, without a word, put the Fiat away. I walked slowly toward the house. I wasn't feeling very brave, but I did think I held the advantage in the event of a showdown which was certainly coming now. If they made no move toward it, I would force their hand.

Ethel met me in the hall. "Didn't know if I should set a place for you, ma'am. I was worried about you."

I smiled serenely and wondered if she was part of the conspiracy. If so, she was playing her part well. "I'll dine with the family."

I heard voices in the drawing room, but I headed for the stairway. In my suite I stretched out on the chaise longue before freshening up for dinner. My stomach was quivering for the ordeal that was fast approaching, yet I had to be careful to present a placid appearance even though a gnawing fear was edging along my spine.

I changed to a jumper and blouse. For the first time, I realized why everything in the closet had a new look to it. I'd not made the purchases, as I'd been told, to please a dying husband. Rather, they'd been made for me and since I was a perfect size ten, there'd been no problem. The shoe size had been taken from the pair I'd worn at the time of the accident. The one error they'd made was in not disposing of the purse with the three keys. No doubt Janet had brought it from the hospital. Or had Dr. Beardsley obtained it with the excuse that he wished to use it to refresh my memory? In any case, Sid had placed it in the safe, never dreaming I'd open the drawer in which it lay concealed. I could imagine their chagrin when they reclaimed the purse from the drawer and found the keys missing. It was then they'd decided to make me believe I was doing things and taking things—like Marilyn's bracelet—and had no memory of doing so.

I thought of Ava and wondered if they'd harmed her.

162

I couldn't believe the story Ethel had told me. That was another thing which would need to be checked.

I would have no more of this sham of making me out to be someone I was not. If it wasn't for the danger they presented to Doug, I might have let it go longer until there was a greater amount of evidence against them. I still didn't know why they'd done this. I had no idea what had happened to the real Sandra Larrabee. I wondered how I'd known so much about the house, but I discounted the slowly growing evidence that I was forgetting things, as if my amnesia was reaching into the present. I knew those incidents of forgetfulness were as unreal as my identity as Sandra. They'd been manufactured and carried out to make me wonder about my own sanity. Part of the pattern of things to come, I supposed. I hoped by tomorrow I'd be out of this house and beginning the search for my true identity.

It occurred to me then that under the pressure of organizing my fight against these people I'd neglected one important fact. I should have looked into the ownership of the car resting under a plastic cover in the garage in Santa Monica as Doug had suggested. The bank officials could likely help me there. I reached for the telephone.

No doubt if I made this call, someone would be listening. It didn't matter to me any more. It was a good way of letting them know the masquerade was at an end. I looked up the number of the bank and made the call.

"This is Mrs. Sandra Larrabee again," I said. "I want a favor of you."

"Anything, Mrs. Larrabee. Please don't hesitate to ask."

"Do you have enough influence with the motor vehicle department, or the police, to get me the ownership of a car to which I have the marker plate numbers?"

"Give them to me and I'll call you back in ten minutes."

"Thank you," I said. "In the event I don't answer the phone or someone says I'm not available, please send someone out here with the name of the owner and be sure to keep a copy for yourself. The messenger must contact me, in person."

"Whatever you wish." I knew from his voice that he was mystified, but he was going to carry out those orders to the letter. If the person operating this scheme had any ideas of doing away with me before the name was delivered, it would be a useless gesture. The bank would deliver that message at any cost. Or, if they found it impossible, they'd be instantly suspicious and take further action. They must have already guessed there was a certain amount of mystery and intrigue about my sudden change of my estate.

I sat by the phone waiting for the call. When it came, the bank manager identified himself.

"I have that information for you now, Mrs. Larrabee. The car is a 1971 Chevrolet Impala, light blue in color, registered in the name of Elizabeth Cawley of Santa Monica."

"Thank you," I said. He had just given me my right name. Elizabeth Cawley! I liked it. Better than Sandra Larrabee, now that I knew I was not Sandra. I was quite likely as poor as Sandra was rich, but I knew I would rather be Elizabeth.

Believing my plans were now carefully laid, I left the suite and went downstairs, holding my head high. My walk was brisk, but I hoped there was a serenity to my manner and my features that revealed none of my inner turmoil.

The family, with the exception of Nancy, was in the dining room. Richie and Sid arose and the former seated me, but not one of the group returned my smile. As if on cue, Ethel entered the room and began serving. It was then I knew Dicie was no longer here. I doubted any of the other servants were either, with the possible exception of the men who patrolled the estate with the dogs. I realized their purpose was to prevent my escape and not as a protection against prowlers.

I also sensed why the twins had been kept from me as much as possible and why they were not, at present, in the house. They might well be at Mrs. Towers', whoever she was. Janet could have requested it and Mrs. Towers obliged. It would be unwise for the twins to be here now. Should there be violence, there must be as few witnesses as possible. And they'd been kept away from me lest they innocently let something slip that would start me thinking and wondering. By the same token, I might reveal something to them that would cast doubts on their belief I was their mother. Carol was the astute one and in the brief time I'd been in their company, I'd noticed her studying me intently. Did she guess there were differences, or was she just bemused that I'd suddenly taken an interest in them?

Richie and Sid were eating their green salad and seemingly enjoying it. Marilyn hadn't touched her's, nor had her eyes left my face. Janet moved the leaves about the plate with her fork, but she seemed to have no appetite for it.

I said, "Why so glum?"

"We're not glum." Janet seemed relieved at the opportunity to speak. "It's just that for the last two days you've kept us on tenterhooks wondering where you've been."

"I was at the hospital. Didn't Dr. Beardsley tell you he saw me there this morning?"

"Yes," she admitted. "He was here about Nancy."

"What's wrong with her?" I asked.

"She's suffered a complete mental breakdown," Marilyn said. "Thanks to you."

"What did I have to do with it?" I made my voice as cold as hers.

"Oh, girls, please," Janet exclaimed. "Not another quarrel."

"I'm sorry, Mother," Marilyn said. "But it seems that since Sandra returned, the air is once again filled with hostility."

"I don't know why," I replied complacently. "The last time I saw Nancy she was very happy at the prospects of a teaching job."

Sid said, "She's too emotionally unbalanced to be a teacher. Besides, she's been drinking too much. Beardsley decided to commit her on a temporary basis to a mental institution until she's dried out. You know she's been drinking."

"Yes," I admitted. "And I think I know why."

Richie set down his fork. "Then suppose you tell us."

"She's frightened—and afflicted with a sense of guilt."

"And why the hell should she be?" he demanded.

"Because she knows I'm not Sandra Larrabee."

Janet's fork dropped to the floor. Marilyn's smile was

ugly. Both men regarded me with new awareness, knowing for a certainty I was on to their game.

Marilyn broke the silence. "Just who are you?"

"Elizabeth Cawley. Didn't one of you listen in on the phone call I got a few minutes ago?"

Sid said, "Yes. It was stupid of me not to destroy that purse."

"And the keys," Marilyn added, a note of disgust in her voice.

He shrugged. "I gambled on the fact Elizabeth would be amenable to our plan. That should her memory return, she'd be so enamored of the luxury she found herself in the midst of, she'd go along with our game. If she didn't, or lost her nerve, I'd confront her with the purse and the keys and use it as a weapon with which she could be destroyed, saying she'd deliberately gone along with it and her amnesia was faked."

Richie said, "It's still a nice life, Elizabeth. You seemed to enjoy the beautiful clothes."

I nodded. "And they seemed very alien to me. I couldn't believe I'd ever been able to purchase such beautiful garments and accessories."

"You weren't," Marilyn said. "But you can if you play it smart. If you don't, you won't have need for a wardrobe of any kind."

Ethel entered the room at that point, with the main course. I said, "Ethel, was it really Ava you took down to the car early this morning, whose struggles awakened me? You told me the cry I heard was when she kicked you in the ankle."

"That's the truth."

"It's a lie," I said. "It was Nancy who was taken from the house. I believe Dr. Beardsley is a part of the conspiracy. He's working in connivance with you. Nancy was drugged early last evening. She was going to tell me the complete story. She wouldn't go along with it any longer. I remember when I told her I was going to make it up to her for my meanness, she replied, 'You weren't mean.' When I asked her what she meant, she refused to elaborate. She was still being loyal to you. She didn't realize the extent of your ruthlessness. That you would even destroy her to keep what you have—this estate and the management of it—or rather the mismanagement. She refused to go along with this terrible game you've been playing with me and she told you so yesterday. I imagine she told you she was going to confess everything to me. For that, you drugged her and with the connivance of Dr. Beardsley, had her committed."

Ethel stood motionless, listening to me, but I saw her features whiten with fear.

I said, "You must have a great deal to gain, Ethel. But you'd better come to your senses. The game is up. They know it. You know it and I know it. In order for me to keep quiet, they'll have to kill me. Your knowledge of that will make you a party to murder. Don't be stupid, Ethel."

"Go to the kitchen, Ethel," Richie commanded. "Never mind the rest of the dinner."

I smiled. "I don't think any of us have much of an appetite. I haven't eaten since breakfast, yet the mere thought of food repels me. Excuse me, please."

I got up, but hadn't reached the door leading to the hall before Sid was at my side, his hand gripping my arm hard.

"I won't try to escape, Sidney," I said. "I know how foolish it would be. I got a good look at those dogs."

Sid nodded. "In that case, we'll go into the drawing room and have a talk."

"About what?" I asked.

"You coming to your senses," he said.

"I may not have my memory," I replied complacently, "but I have my senses."

The others followed and formed a tight group around me as we seated ourselves in the drawing room.

Richie said, "We didn't gamble on your being so intelligent—or falling in love with a snoopy doctor."

I nodded. "He was the catalyst that set this whole thing off. You feared him so much you tried to kill him."

Marilyn registered her disgust with, "That stupid Gilbert had to muff it."

Sid said, "I knew I should have attended to it."

The peal of the doorbell interrupted the talk. Ethel passed by the door and a moment later Dr. Beardsley entered the room. His eyes took in the scene. From their faces he knew there was no longer need to resort to subterfuge.

"How much does she know?" he asked.

Sid said, "We haven't found that out yet. Suppose you tell us, Elizabeth."

I scanned the group, even managing a smile. I was glad the doctor couldn't take my pulse, for he'd find it racing. But thus far, though I was well aware of my peril, I was still in command of the situation and would be so long as I kept them in suspense. Only Dr. Beardsley remained standing and he was pacing back and forth before us.

"Do sit down, Doctor," I urged. "You're a distraction."

His mouth opened to say something, then compressed. Reluctantly, he sat on the settee between Janet and Richie. Marilyn and Sid sat on the one opposite. I was on the ottoman between them, giving me small chance for escape.

Richie said quietly, "Are you going to tell us what you know or must we force it out of you?"

"I'm eager to tell, now that I have your attention," I said. "Just sit quietly until you hear the story."

"For God's sake, get on with it," Richie exclaimed.

"First of all," I said, "you, Sidney, are no longer empowered to handle any part of the estate. Your power of attorney has been cancelled. The bank is now trustee of the estate with legal documents empowering them to handle everything, including a careful audit of the books you've been keeping."

Sidney jumped to his feet and practically ran from the room. I could hear him dialing.

Janet said, "I wish you hadn't done that. I dislike violence, but you leave us no alternative."

Sidney returned. "She's not bluffing. They're still working at the bank taking stock of the estate."

"Don't worry," Dr. Beardsley said. "Elizabeth is going to take care of everything for us. As Sandra, she can revoke these authorizations and return things to their status quo. In fact, it's rather well she did this, because when she does revoke her deal with the bank, she'll be considered somewhat irrational, shall we say?"

I said, "Before you begin the inquisition, may I add that the bank is also in possession of a document in which

168

I have written everything I know about this. They will read it if I am incapacitated, vanish, or turn up dead. I cannot and will not rescind that document."

"I think you can," Marilyn said coldly. "At least we can make you want to try."

"I won't be intimidated, Marilyn."

Richie moved into the conversation. "Elizabeth, why be difficult? There's enough in it for us all. More than enough. We'll gladly grant you a fair portion of profits."

"I'll go along with that," Sidney said.

"No," I said. My fear was growing, but I still managed to conceal it.

"Do something!" Marilyn cried out angrily. "How long are you going to let this go on? Once the bank realizes. . . ."

"Quiet," Sidney said. "Elizabeth, how much do you know? And what are your terms?"

"First, tell me where the real Sandra Larrabee is."

"She's dead!" Marilyn shouted, already evidencing fear of exposure. "You will be too. . . ."

"Shut up." Sidney silenced her.

"My dear," Janet said, "we didn't kill her. I swear we've harmed no one."

"Yet," Marilyn chimed in, significantly.

Sidney walked over, struck her a hard blow across the face. "I told you to keep quiet."

"Sidney, don't," Janet begged. She went over and put a comforting arm around her daughter. "As I was saying, Elizabeth, the real Sandra was never a strong person as far as character was concerned. She was an alcoholic. That's why Larry put Sid in charge of the estate, because she was incapable of handling it."

"How did she die?"

"We had her shadowed. She purchased an around-the-world cruise, but she discovered we knew about it. Fearing we might try to stop her, she booked herself on another ship under another name and evaded the detective. During the cruise she either fell overboard or jumped. Her body was not recovered. We learned of this from a newspaper item and we know it was Sandra from the description given of her."

"There being no record of her death as Sandra Larrabee," I said, "you were safe to produce another Sandra. Did I resemble her so much?"

"It's uncanny," Richie said. "And since Sandra was an alcoholic, she rarely went about with Larry. Besides, she really did come from New York and really was the secretary of a friend of Larry."

"And paid little attention to the twins," I said. "Therefore, passing me off as their mother wasn't too difficult."

Janet sighed. "I'm afraid Carol has doubts. That's why we had to keep them away from you. But our friends saw so little of you, they never questioned it. At the party, we placed two old couples at your table whose sole interest was in the food on their plates. But I want no violence, please."

Marilyn shook herself free of her mother's arm. "For God's sake, let's get on with it."

"I'd like to know what part Dr. Beardsley played in this," I said.

He looked pleased at the question. "I saw you in the hospital almost every day and each time I kept wondering where I'd seen you before. When I realized your resemblance to Sandra Larrabee, I came here and told them about it."

"Have you been friends for long?" I asked.

"Acquaintances," he said. "But we're friends now."

I nodded understandingly. "Once Janet saw me and told the other members of the family, they made a deal with you."

He smiled. "That doesn't concern you."

I returned the smile, though I felt I should fear him as much as any of them. "It concerns me a great deal."

Marilyn pounded the seat cushion with her fists. "Beat her. Make her see reason. Bribe her. Do anything, but get her on our side."

Sid eyed me thoughtfully. "Maybe I *should* use a little physical persuasion."

"Violence won't be necessary," Dr. Beardsley said. "I'm a psychiatrist, remember? I know the human mind and how it functions. I know Elizabeth's mind very well."

"Of course," Marilyn exclaimed. "Hypnotize her again. She does anything you say. She'll convince the bank she made a mistake."

"Hypnotize . . . ?" I cried out. Now the answers to several of my unasked questions were evident.

"No . . . no," Dr. Beardsley said, "that won't be necessary now. I prepared for this once you warned me she and her doctor were snooping and probably were on to us. So I took precautions, which none of you had the foresight to do."

"What precautions?" Sidney demanded.

"Elizabeth, do you recall our little talk in the lounge at the hospital?"

"Yes," I said, and held my breath. Beardsley was too sure of himself.

"Do you recall that I brought your attention to my diamond ring? It flashed in the sunlight."

"You hypnotized me," I said in fresh horror.

"Yes. I'd hypnotized you several times during your stay in the hospital. Once Janet identified you and had me put on the case, it was easy. You gave your consent and were a willing subject. Today, I gave you a pill and told you to put it in your purse. I told you what to do with it, then gave you a post-hypnotic command to go back to Dr. Lansing's room. Next, I ordered a pill sent up to Lansing at once, with orders it was to be used at bedtime. Nobody questioned my authority to do this since I said you'd requested I be put on the case. The pill was delivered, was it not?"

"Yes," I said in a barely audible voice.

"You accepted it. I saw you from the corridor, and while no one watched—you were told to be sure of that— you substituted the pill I gave you for the one the nurse delivered. And that one, Elizabeth—the one you left for him to take—was poison."

I stood up, but Sidney quickly blocked my path, his smile triumphant.

"Well now, it seems we've got you where we want you, Sandy," he said. "This man you've fallen in love with is going to die unless you contact him or the hospital. And you can be assured we won't let you—unless you contact the bank and call off the whole deal. How about it?"

I tried bluffing. "I don't recall being hypnotized."

"Surely," Dr. Beardsley said, "you recall I subjected you to hypnotism in trying to bring back your memory."

"That was days ago. . . ."

"You're a good subject," he said. "You did everything I commanded. You don't recall my hypnotizing you in the lounge. Do you recall my bringing you to this house on three different occasions?"

"I don't recall," I said. I wasn't successful in keeping the quaver out of my voice.

"I can prove I did. While you were under hypnosis, I told you about certain things in this house that you were to remember at a later date. We allowed the twins to see you, though you did not see them. They were told you were their mother and that you'd been sick. They accepted it because you do resemble Sandra uncannily. You remembered what you were commanded to remember. It puzzled you when you finally came here to live and you thought a portion of your memory was returning. You must know. I took you out of the hospital with permission to drive you around to see if you could recall streets and places. The hospital has a record. I'm telling you the truth."

"I believe you," I said.

"Then you have to believe that almost any time now Lansing is going to be administered the poisoned pill. He will die within two minutes after he swallows it."

"Since you ordered the pill, you will be held responsible."

"There is a record of the pill sent to him. It will be proven harmless. An investigation will reveal you were the only outsider admitted to his room, other than hospital staff who will be exonerated."

"What motive would I have for murdering him?"

Dr. Beardsley smiled. "I understand the police believe the accident was a deliberate attempt to murder Dr. Lansing."

"Yes," I said.

"Dr. Lansing recognized you as a fraud," Dr. Beardsley said.

"I'll admit I was here under false pretenses, though due to my amnesia and your hypnotism and suggestion that I was Sandra Larrabee."

"You were blackmailing the family, forcing them into accepting you. Somehow, you learned about the estate—

should the bank uncover the misappropriations. You convincingly faked your amnesia and forced your way into this home. You murdered Dr. Lansing because he attempted to expose you."

"You, a doctor, would resort to murder?" I could no longer hide my terror.

"When I've been promised a million dollars, I'm capable of anything," he said. "Marilyn, take Elizabeth to her room and get the handbag she carried this afternoon. Don't open it. In fact, give it to Elizabeth to bring down."

"Go on," Sidney ordered. "I don't know what it's about, but do as the doctor says."

Marilyn seized my arm and started to pull me. I shook off her grip. "That's unnecessary," I said. "Neither of us will try to get away from here, though you have more reason to than I."

"You're not going to leave here ever," she said angrily.

"We were to bring down the handbag," I reminded her. "It has something to do with poison left in Dr. Lansing's room. If he happens to take it and dies, you won't get the slightest cooperation out of me, so I'd advise you to hurry."

In two minutes we were back in the drawing room. Dr. Beardsley told me to open the bag, which I did. He told me to look in the change purse and hand him the white pill I would find there. I obeyed. He took the pill which, to my knowledge, I had never seen before.

"This," Dr. Beardsley rolled it between his fingers, "is a harmless sleeping pill which was to be administered to Dr. Lansing routinely. This is the pill delivered to him for which you substituted the poison. If I were lying, you have enough intelligence to realize you'd have known about this pill being in your purse, but you did not. It could only have been placed there by you alone, under hypnosis."

I sat down and regarded my tightly clasped hands. Utter defeat flowed through me.

"You will now call the bank officials and tell them you have changed your mind," Dr. Beardsley said. "There may not be much time."

EIGHTEEN

No matter what happened to me, I could not let Doug die. I had to give in to their demands even though it meant I would die. They were gathered about me like a pack of wolves, waiting to move in the moment my confidence and courage waned.

It was not quite eight o'clock. The chances of Doug being given that pill at this early hour were remote. I could gamble a while longer.

Outside it had grown dark, for this was the winter season and the days were short. I arose and, without looking at them, I began pacing the floor as if in deep thought. They watched me intently, knowing I no longer had the upper hand. My hands, at my sides, kept clenching and unclenching, visible evidence of my mental anguish. They watched quietly. Even Marilyn's agitation had vanished. Gradually, I extended my pacing route until I was now fairly close to the exit from the drawing room and reasonably close to the reception hall and the front door.

I paused, halfway back to them, and my eyes shifted to each member of the family, beseeching them for mercy.

Dr. Beardsley's head moved slowly from side to side in a negative manner. Only Janet lowered her eyes.

Sid said, "Don't take too long to think about it."

Dr. Beardsley said, "She won't. She knows what's at stake."

I covered my face with my hands, then dropped them to my sides and resumed my pacing. I was facing the hall and this time, instead of turning around, I tensed momentarily, then sprinted for the front door. Sidney shouted a warning for me to stop, but I paid no heed to it. I reached the door, pulled it open. Ethel, drawn from the kitchen by the noise, tried to stop me, but I was too fast for her. I was outside the house. I felt a surge of freedom and hope. If I could reach Sunset Boulevard with its heavy traffic, I could attract someone's attention. I went racing for the driveway.

They were after me. How many I didn't know because the darkness had closed in around me. I kept going, terror making me fleet of foot, inspiring me to exert myself to the utmost.

I was halfway to the gate when a gray shadow came out of the darkness with what seemed to be the speed of a bullet. At the time I heard the ominous growl in the throat of one of the sentry dogs.

I veered to my right, cut across the grass. The dog had leaped at me, but missed and was now circling to pick me up again. He bayed once or twice and the other sentry dog came loping toward me. I couldn't reach the gate, I could not get back to the house, and there was nowhere on this estate, however remote, where I could evade these especially trained beasts.

One of them nipped at my leg, tearing the bottom part of my dress. In another second one of them would leap on my back and knock me to the ground. Just ahead of me I saw the beginning of the rose arbors. The arches were high, well beyond the limits of these dogs to jump. If I could reach them . . . if I had but a few more seconds. . . .

One dog leaped, baring his teeth in an effort to get my arm in his massive jaws. I managed to escape him. I did reach the first arbor and I grasped barbed branches, pulled myself up and secured a foothold on some sort of crossbeam in the arch. I hauled myself up further.

Below me the dogs barked and growled and kept leaping in an effort to get at me, but I was safely above them now. Safe from the dogs, but helplessly trapped.

The first person to arrive was one of the guards. It wasn't Mike Thornley, the one I'd talked with, so it had to be Tod Briskin.

"Mr. Briskin?" I called out.

"Yes, ma'am." He was already hooking the leash onto the collar of the dog. I heard the sounds of the others running. The guard called out, "She's over here."

"So you're in their pay too," I said.

"Yes, ma'am."

"And the other guard?"

"No, but he was given the night off. I was told you might try a getaway."

"Thanks to you, I didn't make it."

Sid came in sight, followed by the others. He said to the guard, "You can go back now. You'll be well paid for your alertness."

Now all hope was gone. They'd never again be tricked by as simple a ruse as the one I'd used. They would likely tie me up.

Dr. Beardsley said, "Come down, Sandra. Your little trick didn't work."

I was trembling with weakness, my hands were torn and bleeding. I suspected my face too had been ripped by the rose bushes.

Janet called to me. "Come down, Elizabeth. Otherwise you're going to be hurt."

"Shake her down, pull the arbor to pieces and let her fall," Marilyn shouted.

"I'm coming down," I said. All I could think of was that precious minutes were passing. Doug's life was still in danger. Sidney seized my arm as I stepped onto the ground. He raised his hand and slapped me hard across the face. I cried out in pain and anguish.

Dr. Beardsley stepped between us. "Don't be an idiot, Sidney. This girl can queer the whole thing and send the lot of us to prison. There's too much at stake to jeopardize it now."

"With her loving young doctor almost at death's door," Sidney said sarcastically, "she'll do our bidding."

"If you touch me again, Sidney, I'll do nothing to help you, because I'm beginning to believe you'll let Dr. Lansing take that poison no matter what I do. I also believe that you intend to dispose of me. So I have little to lose, while you have everything."

"You shouldn't have slapped her," Janet said. Her tone verged on anger. "We've never even told her what she'll gain by helping us."

"And what she can lose if she doesn't," Marilyn added significantly.

"Oh God, no," Janet moaned. "I wish I weren't a party to this."

Dr. Beardsley led me back to the house, followed by the others. Marilyn addressed her mother. "It's too late to chicken out now."

"You were fortunate, Elizabeth," Richie said mildly, when we were again in the drawing room. "Those dogs could have torn you to pieces. That's what they were trained for."

"Which gives me an idea if Elizabeth refuses to help us," Sidney said. "Heiress, recent victim of amnesia, roaming aimlessly around her estate, killed by her own sentry dogs. That's how the newspapers would start their story."

I repressed a shudder and tried to remain calm. "Before I agree to talk, I want to call Dr. Lansing to be certain he's all right."

"No." Sidney refused my request. "I don't care what the rest of you think, but she's not going to get the chance to warn him. If he finds out about that poison pill, our hold on her is gone. Right now she's risking the life of the man she says she's in love with. Let's see how strong that love is."

"What makes you think the bank officials will still be where we can reach them?" I asked.

"Because I told them to stand by, even if it meant staying there all night. There are millions involved and the bank will profit handsomely, which means the officials will likely get generous bonuses. They'll be there when we want them. But Dr. Lansing won't be, let me warn you."

"Sidney, please," Janet pleaded. It was almost as if she was losing her taste for the scheme.

"Be quiet," Sidney said. "You think this is just some routine business and if we hold out a lollipop to this girl, she's going to do what we say. It won't work that way. She's a stronger character than we bargained on, but not as strong as my determination to break her down. Elizabeth, are you going to listen to reason?"

I said, "Tell me this. Did you kill the real Sandra? I want Janet to answer. I think I can believe her."

"We did not," her answer came promptly. "The private detective we hired kept a close watch on her. But apparently not close enough. She disappeared while on board. She used a fictitious name and nothing she carried bore any identification. She was clever."

"But her very cleverness worked in our favor," Sidney said. "I continued to run the estate."

"And loot it," I said.

"We have extravagant tastes," he said.

"But the estate belongs to the twins," I said.

"There will still be enough for them," Marilyn said. "In the meantime, why should we deprive ourselves?"

Janet said, "It is true that Sandra was an alcoholic. It's also true that even before Larry died, she'd disappear for days and weeks at a time. And true too, that when she returned, she was garbed in cheap, even dirty clothes. We don't know where she went or lived and I don't want to know. Also, she was a tyrant. She found out Sid was appropriating money and ordered us out of the house."

Richie said, "This fortune she inherited from Larry should have been mine to begin with. We were only taking what belonged to us."

"In other words," I said, "each of you is a party to looting the estate. If Sandra was declared dead and the estate went into probate, your thievery would have been discovered. With me taking Sandra's place, you saw a chance to keep the estate to yourselves."

"We still can," Sidney said. "All you have to do is return the authority to me, continue living here as Sandra Larrabee. You were accepted. We took a great risk having that dinner party, but we had to know if you would be accepted as Sandra. Not one person noticed the difference. A few said you'd lost weight, but otherwise you're a dead ringer for our late relative."

"I am to continue to pose as Sandra Larrabee and everything will go on just as before," I said.

"You can even marry your doctor," Janet said.

"I'm against it," Marilyn said. "It's too dangerous. All she has to do is open her mouth and we're finished. She can hold that over us too. I, for one, don't wish to depend on her. She'd be worse than Sandra."

"I don't agree," Sidney told his wife. "I think Elizabeth would go along in return for the life of her young doctor. I say, if she agrees to cooperate, we'll settle the whole thing tonight."

"We'd better," Richie said. "Before the bank uncovers incriminating evidence against us."

Dr. Beardsley added his weight to the argument. "Be sensible, Sandra. The whole thing is foolproof."

"Are we going to sit here all night?" Marilyn asked bitterly. "Besides, if we do wait and Dr. Lansing takes that pill, we're lost. She'll never cooperate."

"That," I said, "is the first sensible thing you've said so far, Marilyn."

"All right." Sidney was growing impatient too. "What's your answer?"

"Why should I trust you after what's happened?" I asked. "What will prevent you from killing me—and letting Dr. Lansing die as well—after I return authority to you?"

"Use your head," Sidney urged. "Even if you return authority to me, if you should die, the whole thing is in the fire again. We'd be lost. We need you alive, to keep up the illusion that Sandra Larrabee lives."

"In fact," Dr. Beardsley said, "I'll see to it that your health remains the finest. You are worth a cool million to me."

"I must then expect to spend the rest of my life living as Sandra. I doubt we can get away with it."

"I know we can," Sidney insisted. "We've already tested that theory and it works. Eventually, you can disappear. Go anywhere you wish. Go back to being Elizabeth

Cawley. That would be a good idea. You'd be declared missing, the estate would eventually be probated and we could swear that you became an eccentric and gave away most of your estate anonymously. We can insinuate that you were not—well—quite sane. Let us worry about that."

"I'm worried we're spending too much time on this," Beardsley said.

"Let me talk to Dr. Lansing," I said.

"Not until after you've asked the bank's lawyers to come here," Sidney told me.

"No," I said.

"My dear girl," Dr. Beardsley pointed out, "if we doublecross you, all you'd have to do is go back on your promise and refuse to change anything when the bank people arrive. We're in this together. It's impossible for one side to outfox the other. From here on, whatever we do has to be mutually agreed upon. Once you get that idea firmly fixed in your mind, you can see that we can't afford to have anything happen either to you or to Dr. Lansing."

He made sense. I didn't trust him any more than I did the others, but he was right in this respect. They couldn't let Doug die without disposing of me. And they needed me.

"I'll make the call," I said. "Immediately afterwards you have to let me talk to Dr. Lansing."

"Agreed," Sidney said. "Of course we can't allow you to tell him what's going on."

"I only want to tell him not to take that pill," I insisted.

"That you may do."

"How will I go about that without arousing his suspicion?" I asked.

Dr. Beardsley said, "I'll call the charge nurse on that floor and tell her I wrote the prescription for someone else, and mistakenly put down Lansing's name because I'd been talking about him to Sandra. They'll believe anything I tell them, and they expect mistakes like that. After all, I'm a very busy doctor."

"I'll make the call," I said. I was too tired to keep arguing. Tired and frightened for myself, horrified to

180

think of the fate Doug might suffer if I delayed too long.

Dr. Beardsley had outwitted me. They held higher cards than I. Maybe they'd kill me afterwards. They might arrange that in a way to satisfy everyone I died by accident, or took my own life. I did have a history of alcoholism and I had likely issued innumerable threats to kill myself. The real Sandra would have done that if I understood her character well enough from what I'd been told about her.

I walked to the nearest telephone.

NINETEEN

Sidney intercepted me and insisted I use the phone in the library, to which he led me, holding onto my arm firmly, though not exerting too much pressure. I was already familiar with the bank's phone number. I made the call and got one of the officials with whom I'd done business this afternoon.

"This is Mrs. Sandra Larrabee," I said. "My brother-in-law has convinced me I've made a serious mistake in removing him as business manager of my estate and revoking the power of attorney under which he has operated for years. I wish you to send representatives to my home at once so the changes can be made. I promise that the bank will be amply paid for all of the work you have so far done and, eventually, you will have the estate to dispose of or to manage. Thank you very much."

"Very well, Mrs. Larrabee," the official said. "Two of us will come to draw up the papers and revoke those you signed this afternoon. I trust you will understand we have spent a great deal of extra time and effort on this business and we are not very pleased with your sudden change of heart."

"A woman," I said, "exerts the privilege of changing her mind. I'll expect you soon."

Sidney hung up the phone. "You handled that well. Now be sensible and go through with the rest of this so that we can all be happy again."

"I will now call Dr. Lansing," I said.

"Not quite yet."

"Unless I am handed that phone in the next minute, I swear to you I will sign no more papers and I'll reveal the full extent of this chicanery. I'm still holding the highest cards, Sidney, and you know it."

He gave me the phone without further protest, except to warn me, "if you say one thing to Lansing about this, I'll snatch that phone from your hand. Do you understand?"

"Yes," I said.

"Come to think of it," he added, "you might tell Lansing that some important circumstances have come up concerned with the return of your memory. Tell him you'll call back late tonight and to please stay awake until you make the call. In that way you can be sure he won't take that pill and we can be sure you won't renege on this deal."

"As you wish," I said. I hadn't expected this much compassion from him, but we were more or less stalemate. We had to bargain. There was no other way out.

I made the call. Much to my surprise, Grace answered. I identified myself and asked, "Aren't you working overtime?"

"The night nurse couldn't make it and the hospital couldn't get anyone else on such short notice, so I'm doing a double shift."

"Thanks, Grace. How is your patient?"

"He was checked over a short time ago and everything is normal. He should be out of here as soon as the broken leg can support him. We're taking him out of traction tomorrow."

"Good, Grace. May I talk to him?"

Doug's voice reached me. It was stronger and guardedly cheerful. "How are things going up there?" he asked. "Or are you calling from the house?"

"Yes. Everything is quiet."

"Who's with you?" he asked.

"I'm alone, Doug." I lied. Sidney nodded heavily in approval.

"Whatever you do, don't let them find out how much you know," he warned me.

"I won't," I replied.

"You don't sound right. As if something is going on, you can't tell me about."

"It's your imagination, darling," I said. "There's nothing to worry about. I'm going to check on that car. When I find out whom it's registered to, I'll call you back and we can discuss it, okay?"

"Great."

"So stay awake, darling. Don't let them give you any sleeping pills or sedation of any kind until after you talk to me."

"I won't."

"Then I'll call you later, in two or three hours. And I'll see you in the morning."

"I'll be here," he said with a dry laugh. "I'm glad everything is under control. Try to keep it that way until I can navigate again. This is a devil of a situation. Did I tell you how it happened? I was driving in answer to a phony sick call—man dying and no other doctor would come. I was moving along pretty fast. This light truck was waiting for me at an intersection of this lonely mountain road. As I rolled by the intersection, it shot out and hit me broadside."

"How awful," I said.

"Whoever is behind all this business won't stop at anything. That's why I'm telling you this. Be careful, darling. Remember, I love you."

"I love you too. Don't worry. I'm quite safe. You'll hear from me shortly."

I hung up. Sidney said, "You handled that well too."

"May I clean up, please? I've been severely scratched and I can feel dried blood on my face. I should look presentable when the people from the bank arrive."

"I'll send Marilyn with you."

"Send Janet. Marilyn is somewhat biased and not in my favor. I might end up with more scratches."

"What do you expect? You've threatened her very way

of life. She's only protecting what she's grown used to. Like all of us."

"Do you think it's worth this much effort and danger?" I asked.

"You bet it is. Think back to what it was like being a librarian. Being paid each month what we spend on an evening's entertainment."

"Was I a librarian?" I asked.

"Yes. I forgot you couldn't remember. But if you could, you'd agree with us."

"Tell me how you found out who I was. I know you did because of what happened at that apartment house in Santa Monica where I used to live."

"We were allowed to search the police missing-persons' lists. The description we found for you also fitted Sandra, of course. They thought we were looking for her. We then did a check on you. If you had close relatives, we weren't going through with it, but you didn't and you fitted our purpose perfectly. Be smart, Elizabeth. Share in the good things of life. Nobody is being hurt. Let's go back to calling you Sandra."

"I shall have to consider it," I said.

"Get cleaned up," he suggested. "You do look somewhat battered. I'm sorry I slapped you. I lost my temper."

I arose and walked up to my suite, followed by Janet. I repaired the damage to my hair and changed into another dress and she sat quietly. I spoke to her twice and drew no answer, so I made no further attempt to communicate with her until just before we went downstairs to wait for the men from the bank.

"Janet, I can sympathize with you in a way. If I'd lived as you did, I'd hate to give it up. I could forgive you for any wrong you did to me, but not for what you've done to Nancy—your daughter."

"She's being cared for."

"In some private institution? As a mental case? She's a sensitive girl. A thing like this could turn her into a genuine mental case. I would hate having that on my conscience."

"What could I do except go along. I want no scandal. Nancy was going to tell you everything. You're the first person she ever trusted. That's what she told us. We

185

couldn't have that. Not until we were sure of you, had you on our side. Please come in with us, Elizabeth. We're not monsters."

"I'd find it hard to live with myself," I said.

"But you will go along—for the time being?"

"Yes. I don't want Dr. Lansing to die."

"I don't either. I wish I'd never become involved. Sometimes I think that when Richie's grandfather left Larry all that money, he did so because he knew it would make trouble. Well, it has. You look very attractive, my dear. And so much like Sandra. I can't get over it."

We went downstairs. The others were seated in the drawing room, all sober-faced. Nobody spoke to me. Their nerves were on edge, but no more so than mine. I felt lost, as if I'd failed myself and Doug. I possessed little doubt but that after I arranged for Sidney to take charge again, and the estate was firmly under his control, that they'd see to it I met with an accident. If they thought Doug knew too much, he too would have another accident and this time there'd be no error.

The only solution I could think of was to go along until I saw a chance to escape, return to Doug and, with his help, try to find a way out. I'd never be in the clear again. If I wasn't threatened with physical violence, they'd say I was in on the deal from the beginning and I'd be as guilty as they in the eyes of the law.

There didn't seem to be any way out for me. No matter which way I turned, I was trapped. Doug's life would always be threatened and so would mine. I felt like bursting into tears, but it was no effort to hold them back. I'd never have allowed these people to see me cry. That's all they'd need to know I admitted defeat.

"A car is coming down the drive," Marilyn announced. She'd been standing by the window, watching for its arrival. "It had better be the bank officials. I'm sick of fooling around."

"Watch to see who gets out," Richie said.

"Two men, with briefcases," she reported. "At least we can be sure of one thing. This doctor lover of her's won't be here."

"Let them in, Richie," Sidney ordered. He glanced at me. "Be calm about this. Apologetic too. You made a mistake. You want to rectify it. That's all there is to this."

"I know," I said.

I heard the door open. Richie didn't greet anyone. When he returned, the two men were behind him and both held not only briefcases, but guns.

"Police," the taller of the pair said. "Which of you is Elizabeth Cawley alias Sandra Larrabee?"

"I'm Elizabeth Cawley," I said.

"Good! The others are under arrest."

Sidney stood up, attempting to bluff, yet knowing very well the game was over. "What's this all about?"

"We're not absolutely certain ourselves," the taller detective replied. "But a girl named Nancy Larrabee has been telling her story to the District Attorney."

Sidney sat down heavily. Richie heaved a great sigh. Marilyn was muttering something under her breath and Janet began to weep. I arose and joined the two detectives. I knew I was now safe.

TWENTY

It was morning before I was able to visit Doug, though I'd talked to him on the phone several times during lulls in the periods when the police and the District Attorney were questioning me.

When I approached his room, the door was open and there were no longer any restrictions on seeing him. He was sitting up in bed, looking quite fit and he greeted me with a warm embrace.

"We had quite a time here after you called," Grace told me. "We didn't know what was happening."

"I can imagine," I said. "I was terrified lest Doug take the poisoned pill."

"It's been checked," Grace said. "It was poison all right."

"Dr. Beardsley hypnotized me yesterday morning in the lounge and put the poisoned pill in my purse. He ordered me to substitute it for the tranquilizer he'd prescribed through the hospital pharmacy. He'd have sworn I asked him to go on the case."

"Under the circumstances, I marvel you came out of

it with your life," Doug said. "But I'm grateful you did. And proud of you."

Grace said, "I'll let you two talk it out. Time for me to go home and get some sleep. If you don't mind, Doctor?"

"Not in the least," he said with a smile.

She gathered up a sweater and her handbag, waved a farewell and went out, closing the door as she did so. Doug held out his hand to me and I sat down in the chair alongside the bed.

"I've been in touch with the District Attorney and the police," he said. "Everything is clear now. This was a fantastic scheme, inspired by Dr. Beardsley, when he saw you here in the hospital and realized how closely you resembled Sandra. Of course there were factors in favor of the scheme. Sandra was a recluse and an alcoholic and people had seldom seen her. If there were minor differences in your appearance and hers, the lapse of time and the accident explained them."

"Did the police tell you Sandra was really drowned at sea?" I asked.

"Yes, but no details."

I told him then all I'd learned from the Larrabees and Dr. Beardsley and how the bank officials had already discovered that Sidney, in connivance with the other members of the family with the exception of Nancy, had looted the estate to a considerable degree. That was why they were delighted when Dr. Beardsley discovered me in the hospital. He had been called to treat Sandra before Larry Larrabee died, though without success. But when he called the Larrabees and told them about me, they immediately offered him a million dollars if he would consent to the scheme they had in mind of me assuming the identity of Sandra Larrabee.

When I completed my story, he told me the police had arrested Gilbert, who admitted he was the driver of the panel truck which struck Doug's car; it had been he who made the call summoning Doug to that deserted mountain road.

Ethel too was a part in the conspiracy, but readily admitted her guilt, hoping for immunity. However, Nancy was the state's best witness. She'd never gone along with

189

the conspiracy and believed, at first, I was a party to it. Only when she was convinced of my innocence, did she threaten the family with exposure. She had told them of my visit to the apartment house, not with the intent of harming me, but in an attempt to force them to admit the truth to me and let me go. When they refused and she was still adamant, threatening to tell me herself, she was given a drink containing a drug. She'd been in a drugged stupor when I looked in on her that night to inform her the family had consented to her teaching.

"There's still one thing that puzzles me," I said. "And I think you know what it is."

"You want to know if I always knew your identity." At my nod, he said, "Not always, but once I learned you were supposed to be the mother of twins, which I knew to be impossible, I set about finding out who you were."

"And how did you accomplish it?"

"The same way the Larrabees did. I checked police missing persons' records and found your description. You'd been reported missing by the head librarian."

"I still haven't my memory back," I said.

"In time you will, because now we know who you are. That practically insures it."

"And I have no relatives?"

"You didn't have," he said with a smile.

"Didn't?" I asked vaguely.

"That's right, but soon you will have. Me. Now isn't that a practical way for a man to ask a girl to marry him?"

I bent down and kissed him. "From you, darling, any way is a good way, but you don't have to be quite that practical, do you?"

"Wait," he said, "until I get out of this hospital."

"Then get well soon, darling."

Doug's recovery was normal. He lost most of his recently built-up practice, but he was unworried about that. The Larrabees were brought to trial under great publicity. The trial itself was brief. They pleaded guilty. A lenient judge gave them probationary sentences, except for Dr. Beardsley and Sidney, who were sent to prison. Gilbert, too, drew a prison sentence for conspiracy and attempted murder.

Nancy was declared perfectly competent. She did an excellent job of convincing the doctors where she'd been committed that there was a conspiracy afoot in her family which had already involved attempted murder. They were still skeptical until she insisted they call Doug. Once they did and learned the facts, the wheels of justice started turning.

She's teaching now and quite normal and happy. A contrite and penitent Janet has been allowed to care for the twins, though they also have a court-appointed guardian. Marilyn has taken an apartment elsewhere, the court forbidding her to live in proximity to the twins.

My memory is slowly returning. Every few days there is another experience which helps to bring it back. Friends I knew, the library where I worked, even the bookstore on Robertson Boulevard where the myopic owner now recognizes me. I had been in the habit of going there to search for rare books the library wanted on its shelves.

Doug's practice will soon be flourishing, for he is a capable doctor. We'll have our own family before long, but that won't keep us from visiting the Larrabee mansion to see Nancy and the twins.

The house doesn't frighten me any more. It is still one of the most splendid homes in Los Angeles, but I had no regrets at leaving it. In the apartment Doug and I gradually furnished as our finances increased, I feel safe and there is more love in those few rooms than there ever was in the Larrabee mansion.